"Dearly beloved, we are gathered...."

Maggie tried to follow the preacher's words and ignore the fact that her hand was tucked in next to Griff's powerfully muscled arm, inches from his heart.

She found herself turned, facing Griff, her hands swallowed in his warm grip. His shadow blocked out the sight and sound of everyone around them, his musky scent filling her senses.

Gooseflesh rose along her arms as she saw both intent and purpose engraved in his hard face and felt the force of his personality.

"You're not going to faint on me, are you?"

Before she could respond, an authoritative voice echoed through the room. "Freeze! Put your hands in the air and don't move!"

Dear Reader,

Once again we invite you to enjoy six of the most exciting romances around, starting with Ruth Langan's *His Father's Son*. This is the last of THE LASSITER LAW, her miniseries about a family with a tradition of law enforcement, and it's a finale that will leave you looking forward to this bestselling author's next novel. Meanwhile, enjoy Cameron Lassiter's headlong tumble into love.

ROMANCING THE CROWN continues with *Virgin Seduction*, by award winner Kathleen Creighton. The missing prince is home at last—and just in time for the shotgun wedding between Cade Gallagher and Tamiri princess Leila Kamal. Carla Cassidy continues THE DELANEY HEIRS with Matthew's story, in *Out of Exile*, while Pamela Dalton spins a tale of a couple who are *Strategically Wed*. Sharon Mignerey returns with an emotional tale of a hero who is *Friend, Lover, Protector*, and Leann Harris wraps up the month with a match between *The Detective and the D.A.*

You won't want to miss a single one. And, of course, be sure to come back next month for more of the most exciting romances around—right here in Silhouette Intimate Moments.

Enjoy!

Leslie J. Wainger
Executive Senior Editor

Please address questions and book requests to:
Silhouette Reader Service
U.S.: 3010 Walden Ave., P.O. Box 1325, Buffalo, NY 14269
Canadian: P.O. Box 609, Fort Erie, Ont. L2A 5X3

Strategically Wed
PAMELA DALTON

Silhouette®

INTIMATE MOMENTS™

Published by Silhouette Books

America's Publisher of Contemporary Romance

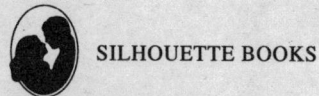 SILHOUETTE BOOKS

ISBN 0-373-27220-0

STRATEGICALLY WED

Visit Silhouette at www.eHarlequin.com

Printed in U.S.A.

Books by Pamela Dalton

Silhouette Intimate Moments

Who's Been Sleeping in Her Bed? #1020
Strategically Wed #1150

Silhouette Romance

The Prodigal Husband #957
Second Chance at Marriage #1100
And Baby Makes Six #1234

PAMELA DALTON

believes in happily-ever-afters. She fell in love with her husband, Mark, through the letters they exchanged while he was stationed in Fort Knox, Kentucky, and she was attending college in Sioux Falls, South Dakota. When he finally flew back for their first "official" date, he popped the question twenty-four hours later, and Pamela said yes. Married to her hero for more than twenty-five years, she cherishes her quality family time with her two adult children, Betsy and Peter.

To Lori Handeland,
Your friendship and support mean so much.

Chapter 1

Maggie Bennington had never had a case of the jitters in her life. She'd always lived her life by her late father's philosophy "show no fear," no matter what was at stake. But then, she'd never been in this position before.

Staring through the short lacy veil covering her face, she glared across the long church aisle to the man waiting at the other end.

It wasn't fair, she thought as she battled another attack by renegade butterflies strategizing for position in her stomach.

For never having done this before, Griff Murdock looked too comfortable in the traditional setting. Too at ease. A man's man. A cop's cop. Nothing could change Griff from what he was. Nothing.

Not even his own wedding with a number of well-dressed guests seated on ribbon-decked pews, watching every move he made.

Dressed in the stark black tuxedo that fit his six-foot-two broad-shouldered frame almost to perfection, Griff was primed and ready, his steel-gray eyes seeing too much and revealing so little. It was part of his attraction. Part of the danger.

That grated, too. Maggie clutched her bouquet of mums. It would have soothed her a bit to witness some sign of agitation on his stoic face, if only to see him rake fingers through his crisply groomed dark hair where tips of gray were starting to appear. Why couldn't he be shifting from one foot to the next or trying to loosen his collar?

She, on the other hand, kept tugging on the neckline of her dress that was threatening to strangle her. Years of training kept her from turning into a hysterical fool. But she wasn't sure how much longer she was going to hold up under the pressure.

"Hey, Maggie," Sergeant Jameson whispered a protest, trying to loosen the death grip she had on his comforting arm. "I still have some use for that particular limb. How am I going to perform my duties if you've blocked all the blood from my arteries?"

"Sorry, Wylie." Maggie tried to unclench her stiff fingers from the solid, reassuring muscle that had been her only anchor on reality since she'd arrived at the church. Berating herself for being such a coward, she shook off her uneasy thoughts and turned to eye the older man at her side.

Wylie, her father's dearest friend and her godfather, had been the logical choice to escort her down the aisle following her father's death a year ago. His wavy silver hair neatly trimmed and gleaming in the muted light, Wylie appeared to be every inch the father of the bride in his elegant wedding attire.

"You look plum scared out of your wits," Wylie said, his shrewd eyes flickering over her pinched features.

"Me? Why should I be scared with a room full of Pendleton's finest surrounding me?"

A bit of deviltry tipped the corners of her godfather's grin. "You're a lucky woman. What other woman has an entire police department watching over her at her wedding?"

She knew Wylie was trying to reassure her and keep her calm. He had always been more of a father to her than her real parent.

For Wylie's sake, Maggie made a serious attempt to raise a smile. Her godfather certainly had enough on his mind right now. He didn't need to worry about her getting cold feet, yanking out all the pins that clamped her wayward red hair into an uncomfortable position and hightailing out the closest door. "Guess I must be having an allergic reaction to wearing high-heeled shoes."

"Getting anxious, are you?"

"Anxious to get out of here."

His blue eyes twinkled down at her. "It'll be finished in an hour or so. That's not so long."

Her designer wedding dress, made up of acres of satin and adorned with hundreds of tiny pearls, didn't make any allowances for breathing. Reaching up,

Maggie yanked on the constrictive high neck of her gown again. "This dress should have come with a warning label. I feel as if I'm wrapped in jewel-studded cellophane."

Wylie clicked his tongue against his teeth. "Serves you right, kitten." Even though the use of his personal nickname for her was said with affection and warmth, the sound lacked any kind of sympathy. "That dress looks like a suit of armor. A little cleavage might have loosened you up a bit."

Conscious of Griff's brooding presence just across the room, Maggie wasn't about to explain her real reason for being cloaked in a dress that shrouded every inch of her figure. "I've provided enough entertainment for the Pendleton Police Department recently without having my bosom on display for everyone to leer at," she said with a shudder.

Wylie chuckled. "Don't get your back up." The gravelly rumble in his voice tried to coax a smile out of her. "We've just been having a bit of fun. You and Griff. Fire and ice. Who would ever have thought we'd see you two march down the aisle together?"

"Yes, who would have thought?"

Fire and ice. She'd overheard the comparison being bantered around the Pendleton Police Department. There had been plenty of other jokes tossed about their supposed mismatch.

It was no wonder the department was gripping their sides with laughter. She couldn't believe it herself.

Maggie wore her heart on her sleeve, whereas Griff was a master at keeping his emotions in lockdown.

Now they would be meeting at the end of her march down that long aisle ahead of her.

Against her will, her gaze found Griff's. Even from this distance, the steel-gray depths beckoned her. Her stomach twisted another half notch. Chills raced up and down her spine, despite the warm September day and stuffiness inside the church as the air between them seethed with a static she couldn't quite categorize—and certainly didn't trust. Could the tension of what lay ahead for them be undermining Griff's infamous control, too? The thought made her even more nervous.

Wylie squeezed her icy fingers. "Might as well enjoy it. A bride is supposed to like all the hype and trimmings."

His welcome interruption gave her the strength to tear her gaze from Griff's. "I can't imagine why."

The older man shook his head, the silver of his hair catching in the light. "Ah, Maggie, my love, where is your sense of romance?"

"Dad always said romance was for fools."

"There are more than a few women who would love to trade places with you. You're one lucky woman."

"And I didn't even have to buy a lottery ticket."

He chuckled. "Nice try, Maggie. I know true love when I see it. Those green eyes of yours can't hide a thing."

True love? Her fingers tightened around the flowers. She didn't dare examine her real feelings for Griff, the department's Golden Boy. Not if she wanted to make her way down that long, long aisle.

The butterflies raising a ruckus in her stomach were already betting against her ability to go through with it.

Who knew what could go wrong? Despite all their planning and preparation—

Stop it, Maggie, she ordered herself. If she backed out, she'd let down not only Griff and Wylie but herself.

And Aunt Jessica.

Oh Lord, just thinking of Aunt Jessica's expectations made her head throb. Her aunt, her father's sister and the only remaining relative Maggie had, was seated at the front of the church, no doubt already dabbing her eyes with one of the three monogrammed handkerchiefs she'd insisted on bringing.

Aunt Jessica adored Griff and always had. She had so many hopes riding on this marriage. She'd fussed over him each time she arrived from Florida for a visit. There was always a Christmas present for Griff along with all the other packages her aunt sent.

Now that they were to be married, her aunt couldn't contain her enthusiasm and delight.

Maggie squeezed her eyes shut and tried to suck in a stress-relieving breath. She'd honor her word, fulfill her commitment and hope for the best. After all, she'd survived tougher situations.

How tough could a wedding be?

Da-a-dum-de-dum.

The sound of the organ chiming the opening notes of the bridal march sent the butterflies inside her hurdling into kamikaze maneuvers.

Wylie snagged her hand through the bend of his arm. ''Look's like the show is about to begin.''

Maggie struggled against the temptation to grab the hem of the suffocating white dress and race out the door. Why hadn't she insisted on a small wedding?

Show no fear, her father's voice echoed through her head.

Maggie clamped down on her cowardliness.

Her gaze rose and locked with Griff's. She saw the challenge in his expression, felt the dare. He knew she was hedging. Her hackles rose as she caught his glint of amusement. Darn him.

She lifted her chin.

Wylie tugged on her arm, his feet moving forward in the formal wedding glide. "Come on, Maggie. Smile."

She didn't respond, using every bit of energy she had to keep track of placing one foot in front of the other.

Remember the timing.

Listen for your cue.

Think about what's at stake.

Keep your chin high.

"Relax," Wylie breathed at her side. "Marie Antoinette probably looked happier walking to the guillotine."

"Is the guillotine an option?" Her smile muscles refused to cooperate. Without looking at Wylie, she could feel his silent laughter. It was easy for him. He wasn't going to pledge "'til death do us part" to Griff Murdock.

Each step echoed a hammering drumbeat in her head and drew her closer to the inevitable. The weight of her fancy hairdo became heavier.

She tried to give herself a pep talk and be grateful she only had to go through this once and then never again. Perhaps women who had their real fathers at their side, with their mothers beaming mistily at them from afar, found some kind of meaning in this pomp and circumstance, but it reeked of phoniness to Maggie. Both her parents were dead, and she was in the midst of cops—the only family she'd ever really had.

Griff's gaze never released hers. Seductive, deep, compelling. Always drawing more from her than she wanted to give. Always knowing. Always seeing.

Did he suspect what she was thinking?

She saw his gaze slip down to her lips. Her insides flip-flopped. Why Griff Murdock of all people?

But then it had always been Griff. Griff, who had attended her high school graduation in place of her father. Griff, who'd sent her flowers after she'd gotten hurt in a sledding accident.

Grappling with her waning courage, Maggie forced her gaze to shift to the darkly robed man standing near the pulpit.

The unfamiliar face of the robed man took a moment to register. She frowned. ''Where's Armstrong?'' she whispered the question through her locked teeth.

''Reverend Foxworth insisted he's the only one who performs weddings in his sanctuary.''

Maggie stumbled. ''Reverend—''

Wylie steadied her, without losing a beat of their pace. ''Don't worry about it. This won't hurt a bit.''

Any argument to the contrary fled the next moment as Wylie thrust her cold fingers into the shocking warmth of Griff's. Touching the live heat radiating from his palm nearly buckled Maggie's knees.

''Going to make a run for it?'' Griff's deep-throated drawl accompanied a sardonic lift to his left eyebrow.

''Only if you do.''

''I love a woman who will follow her man anywhere.''

His low-pitched banter helped her relax. She tossed her veiled head, ignoring the screaming protest of her tightly bound hair. "Who's following?" she whispered loud enough for the preacher to hear. "I'm using you to blaze the trail in front of me."

The pastor cleared his throat noisily and gave them both a stern look laden with disapproval before saying,"Dearly beloved, we are gathered..."

Drawing a mask over her features, Maggie tried to follow the preacher's words and ignore the fact that her hand was tucked in next to Griff's powerfully muscled arm, inches from his heart.

The thought did little to settle her uneasiness.

A heart was not something she'd ever associated with Griff.

"Repeat after me..."

She found herself turned, facing Griff, her hands swallowed in his warm grip. The late afternoon sun beamed through the kaleidoscope of church windows, forcing her to squint into his face. His shadow blocked out the sight and sound of everyone around them, his musky scent filling her senses.

Gooseflesh rose along her arms as she saw both intent and purpose engraved in his hard face and felt the force of his personality.

Surrealism descended over her as Griff recited his vows first.

Then it was Maggie's turn. Her voice sounded strange, totally foreign, a testimony to the tightness that lodged in her throat. Somehow she managed to respond, only stumbling once.

The reverend nodded to her. "Give Griff your left hand."

Apprehension slithered up Maggie's backbone.

Handing her bouquet jerkily to Christine, a fellow officer and her only attendant, Maggie turned to face Griff again. Without looking directly into his face, she thrust her hand toward him.

The ring slid smoothly into place.

Then Christine reached over and gave Maggie the groom's ring. Maggie tried to keep her hand steady as she recited the short vows while holding Griff's finger and trying to maneuver the gold band.

The ring hit a major roadblock at Griff's knuckle.

Before she could release his finger and let him complete the task, his warm, dry hand closed over hers and helped her slide the ring past the ridge. She forgot to breathe. Trapped close to his side, she understood how a prisoner felt when the handcuffs were snapped on and he saw his freedom slip away.

"You're not going to faint on me, are you?" The growl in Griff's voice made her straighten.

She shot him a rebuking look, noticing that while his words contained their usual teasing, his gray eyes were sober.

Before she could respond, an authoritative voice echoed through the room, "Freeze! Put your hands in the air and don't move!"

Chapter 2

Griff reacted on gut instinct.

"Everyone down on the floor," he shouted over his shoulder.

He shoved Maggie behind the pulpit and came down heavily on top of her. Her outraged gasp boded ill, but he didn't take time to apologize. He was more concerned no bullets separated their heads from their bodies.

From the corner of his eye, he could see the pews were cleared.

The only movement came from the twisting woman beneath him. He hadn't been with a woman for almost a year, and his body responded instantly to the feel of Maggie's silky limbs entwined with his. Gritting his teeth, he attempted to block out his own discomforts and pinpoint the exact location of where the police command had come from. The order had been muffled, most likely originating from someplace inside the church but outside the sanctuary.

Maggie thrust her hands between their bodies and tried to push him away. "What do you think you're doing?" she whispered furiously, her voice distorted by the veil smothering her face. She squirmed beneath him, barely missing a strategic part of his body with her lethal knees.

He cursed and rolled away.

Sparing her a quick glance, he saw her swatting at the veil and trying to untangle herself from the swathing of cloth that had hiked up around her hips and become partially snagged between her legs.

Maggie yanked her dress from under his weight but not before he caught sight of her creamy thighs.

Griff gritted his teeth and swallowed hard. He didn't need this kind of distraction right now.

He forced his gaze away and reached around her to pull his gun from the ledge inside the pulpit. "Can you take it from here?" he asked shortly.

She shot him a dirty look and grabbed her own gun that had been hidden there as well. "Next time you wear the dress, and I'll wear the pants," she retorted.

"I love it when you get kinky, Bennington."

"Put a sock in it, Murdock."

The spitting fury on her face told Griff it would be best to remove himself from the proximity of Maggie's dangerous knees and deadly trigger finger. A smart man didn't tangle with a woman holding a gun—especially one who could handle a gun better than most men he knew. There was one thing everyone agreed upon about Griff Murdock: he was a smart man.

With another quick look over his shoulder, he sprinted over the altar and slipped into the doorway of the small room next to the sanctuary. From his vantage point, he saw the pews were now clear of all their occupants. There didn't seem to be any immediate danger, but appearances could be deceiving.

The pastor, who was hidden behind the choir loft with the organist, gave Griff a questioning look. Griff motioned for him to stay put and try to quiet the organist, who was obviously having trouble catching her breath.

From the corner of his eye, he saw Wylie nod to him just before the older man slipped out the back door. Several other officers, moving with stealth and caution, found their way to a side door off to his left before disappearing down the basement stairs to check out the lower floor.

Outside, sounds of a door slamming and several shouts reverberated through the stone walls as Griff braced himself for any unexpected movements or noises. An unnatural hush reverberated through the sanctuary. There hadn't been any shots fired, but he knew better than to relax his vigilance.

Waiting was his least favorite part of being a cop, but at least this ritual was a more comfortable scenario than the one he'd been performing just moments earlier.

Griff scanned the church again, his head steeped with Maggie's seductive scent, which had teased him throughout the brief ceremony. He couldn't remember being so distracted, and that wasn't a good situation for a cop to be in. But lately, he'd had difficulty keeping his mind on the job. Since Maggie had returned to the police department, he'd found himself hungry for something he couldn't name.

Griff tried to shake off his tangled thoughts. He'd be glad when they wrapped this up and he could get out of this monkey suit.

Scouring the big room again, the only movement Griff could detect came from the three big fans hanging from the vaulted ceiling. Their whirring efforts to cool failed to provide any relief as rivers of sweat meandered down his neck and seeped through his tuxedo.

A funeral-like silence emanated from the people trapped under the pews. Everyone seemed to be holding their breaths except for the organist, who was crouched near the pastor and whose big bosom heaved with hysteria, vocalized by ragged whimpers. The reverend awkwardly patted her shoulder as his attempts to hush her proved fruitless.

Griff caught Maggie's eye. With a steady hand on her firearm, she shifted soundlessly closer to the choir loft. With her empty hand she reached out and touched the frightened woman's arm.

"Please stay calm, ma'am." Maggie's voice was low but firm. "Everything is under control. This will be all over in a minute. We're just taking precautions."

Griff noticed the organist's big heaving sobs instantly ebbed.

Maggie had a natural way of dealing with people,

something that Griff could appreciate since he didn't have the patience to baby-sit. His superiors claimed he was too abrupt, repeatedly lecturing him to be more politically correct—whatever the hell that meant. He frankly didn't care. He refused to reason with the unreasonable while a ticked-off husband emptied his shotgun into someone's back. From Griff's point of view, that's how too many people ended up dead.

Still in this dicey situation, he appreciated Maggie's rapport with the organist. She had just the right touch as well as a delectable body. The lower part of his anatomy still hummed with the memory of her seductive squirming. His wayward thoughts instantly formed pictures of illicit, steamy wedding night images.

Cool it, Murdock. The last thing he could afford to do right now was forget the task at hand and obsess over Maggie's desirability as a woman. He had to keep his mind alert and focused.

A shout outside forced his thoughts back to the matter at hand. He exerted his iron control in reclaiming his wayward thoughts as the moments stretched and lapsed.

After what seemed to be a lifetime that taxed all Griff's reserves, Wylie's face appeared in the doorway. "Okay, folks. You can get up now."

A gust of sighs resounded as people emerged from their crouched positions and began to talk. Wylie had to raise his voice to be heard. "I want everyone to walk single file through the doors and down the basement. Please show the officers in the back some identification with your name and address."

Maggie stood up, staggering slightly as her heel caught on the edge of the dress. Ugh! She couldn't wait to escape this shroud and the stuffy confines of the church.

"Mrs. Murdock, is everyone okay?" Reverend Foxworth asked her as he helped the quaking organist to her feet.

Maggie chose to ignore the Mrs. Murdock salutation for now. There wasn't time for explanations at this point. "Everyone seems to be fine, Reverend."

The pastor turned away.

Hitching up the hem of her dress so she wouldn't trip over it again, Maggie slipped as quickly as she could through the crowd before arriving at Wylie's side. "Everything go down okay?"

"Like clockwork." His earlier affability had completely disappeared. In its place he'd donned the unemotional professionalism that had earned him the respect of every officer in his department. "The sting went exactly the way we planned it. We nabbed two of them."

Some of Maggie's tension eased. She reached back and worked the tight muscles at the base of her neck, trying to loosen the stress. "Who did you collar?"

"A woman and a man who was dressed like a woman. They don't appear to be anybody local. Both have those weird Eastern accents."

"Anyone else?" Griff asked, appearing behind them, looking too calm for Maggie's taste and making her feel even more rumpled than she already was.

Wylie frowned, keeping a close eye on the people standing together in groups. "We're looking at some suspicious footprints under an open window in the back. But some kid who wanted to check out the scene might have made them. The video equipment McDuff rigged up outside the church should be able to tell us if there was anyone else working this job. McDuff swore we'd get anything that moved, even squirrels scavenging nuts for the winter. But just to be on the safe side, we need to check out the guests in case they had someone planted inside.''

''What do you want us to do?'' Maggie asked.

''Station yourselves at the end of these aisles. Make a note of anyone you don't recognize.''

As Wylie walked away, Griff turned and looked at her. ''You okay?'' he asked.

She nodded. ''I'd love to escape this dress.''

''You don't have to keep wearing it on my account,'' he drawled, his gaze sweeping her body from head to toe.

Maggie couldn't stop the blush surging past her neckline. ''You're dreamin','' she said coolly.

Griff chuckled, surprising her by catching her chin with his index finger. ''You make a beautiful bride. I wish BJ could have been here to see you.''

Without waiting to hear her response, he gave her a wink and left.

His comment sucked the wind from Maggie's lungs. His little zingers throughout the brief service had been familiar and safe.

But this had been personal.

What had Griff meant by his comment? Over the past two months of their whirlwind engagement, they'd skillfully steered clear of BJ's name. Why had he brought up her father now?

Maggie's gaze followed Griff's long powerful strides down the aisle. He'd already resurrected his professional façade. He did it so masterfully.

That realization made her stiffen her backbone. She gathered the long skirt of her gown and moved toward the other corner of the sanctuary. She didn't have time to worry about Griff's cryptic comments now.

Fortunately, everyone cooperated. Maggie didn't spot any mysterious strangers among the people parading slowly by her. Since most of the guests were cops, she easily identified their names or faces. She exchanged greetings with a few.

By the time she was finished, her back and feet ached in too many places to count. With the setting sun gleaming through the colorful windows and casting a golden reflection on the cherrywood pews, she searched the empty sanctuary and realized she was the only person left in the large, hollow-sounding room.

Griff had disappeared, too.

For a brief second she allowed herself the luxury of contemplating the relief of getting out of this perspiration-laden dress and escaping into a tub of bubbles. But she knew she'd have to postpone her indulgence just a little while longer. Wylie and Griff would be waiting for her final report. Then she could leave.

Slipping off her shoes, Maggie followed the sound of voices and descended the basement steps. Pushing open the door she found the rest of the department and guests. Reception food had been spread out on the tables, and the people milling around were eating or chatting. The earlier tension had evaporated. Any person wandering in off the street would never have believed anything out of the ordinary had taken place earlier. To all intents and purposes, everyone looked like they were celebrating the aftermath of a wedding.

Before she could cross the room to Wylie, Aunt Jessica, all decked out in a new rose-covered dress and clutching her handkerchief to her bosom, emerged from a cluster of people.

"Maggie, I don't understand any of this," Jessica wailed in typical Jessica-fashion, latching on to Maggie's arm. "Why did they ruin your wedding with this police nonsense?"

Maggie placed an arm around her aunt's shoulders and gave her a gentle hug. "This wasn't a real wedding, Aunt Jessica. It was a sting operation. I'm sorry I couldn't tell you the truth."

It pained her to see her aunt's expression go from a state of confusion to disbelief. "You mean someone planned to use your wedding to play cops and robbers?"

Maggie had been dreading this confrontation ever since her aunt, who was now a full-time resident in a Florida retirement village, had arrived on Maggie's doorstep a week ago.

Eyeing her aunt's set expression, Maggie knew explaining the real intent and purpose of the wedding wasn't going to sit well with a woman who delivered a Valentine to her dead husband's grave every February. Still, her aunt knew what it meant to have a cop in the family. BJ, Jessica's brother and Maggie's father, had always put the job first.

Maggie pulled out a chair for her aunt. "Why don't you sit down while I explain."

Her aunt folded her arms stubbornly. "I'd prefer to stand."

Maggie noticed Griff move a chair next to her aunt and nudge the older woman gently into the seat. Jessica didn't protest. She turned and grabbed his hand. "BJ always wanted you to marry Maggie, you know."

Griff hunched down next to her. "I know, but BJ would have wanted us to put these guys out of business first."

"What guys?"

Maggie pulled a chair forward and faced her agitated relative. "Aunt Jessica, do you remember when the state senator's daughter was robbed at her wedding four months ago? That robbery was one of fifteen heists pulled off during the past eighteen months in a three state area. The thieves had a pretty lucrative thing going. They'd simply walk into the church while the wedding was going on, rifle through the wedding party's personal belongings and filch whatever cash and credit cards they found. They also looted the wedding gifts. We set up this sting to put these guys out of business."

The older woman's disbelieving gaze slipped to Griff and then back to Maggie. She shook her head vehemently. "But you both had blood tests taken."

"We had to. We didn't know how the thieves picked their victims. They might have been checking applications for wedding licenses or perhaps they were checking bridal registries at the major department stores. Every part of the wedding had to look real.''

Her aunt lifted her double chin to a level that made it seem she was looking down at them. ''You recited your vows in front of a man of God and in a church.''

Maggie was starting to feel the full weight of their deception.

Griff came to her rescue. ''During the last wedding the thieves hit, they assaulted and robbed a guest who slipped into a rest room during the service. The woman nearly died.''

Jessica paled. ''And what if someone had gotten hurt here?''

''Reverend Foxworth, the organist and you were the only civilians,'' Maggie said, as gently as she could. ''We secured the sanctuary so none of you were in danger.''

Reverend Foxworth suddenly appeared at Jessica's elbow and the older woman glared at him. ''How could you agree to this charade?''

He shook his head. ''This is the House of God. God has never taken kindly to money changers or looters invading His domain. I figure He had a hand in nailing these sinners.''

Before anyone could comment, a twinkle entered his eye, and he added, ''Of course, He probably would be all in favor of these two fine people formalizing their union. All we need are their signatures on the dotted line of the marriage certificate. I've officiated less promising unions.''

Maggie attempted to control a grimace. ''Reverend,

we appreciate all your help, but your job is over as far as I'm concerned.''

For a moment her aunt didn't comment, using the silence to impose her will.

When it became evident she couldn't change the inevitable, Jessica released a sigh of futility and turned her back on the pastor. She eyed Maggie wistfully. ''You've been alone all your life, my dear. I only wanted for you to have what my Harold and I had.''

''I know,'' Maggie said softly.

Maggie's own mother had died within days of Maggie's birth. Jessica was the closest person Maggie had to a mother.

Maggie would never intentionally hurt or mislead her aunt. Unfortunately, one of Aunt Jessica's friends had gotten wind of the wedding and had alerted her aunt.

Aunt Jessica's surprise arrival nearly destroyed the entire plan. Telling her aunt the truth had been out of the question because everyone knew Jessica couldn't keep a secret. More than once Maggie considered calling a halt to the whole thing. She had only agreed to continue with the wedding charade after Griff and Wylie arranged to have someone whisk her aunt out of the sanctuary and into a side room as soon as the robbery went down.

Jessica's chin quivered. ''You *really* aren't getting married?''

''I'm sorry, Aunt Jessica,'' Maggie said.

She couldn't blame her aunt for being disappointed. But Maggie didn't really believe in happily-ever-after—not with a cop. And especially not with Griff.

Disappointment filled Jessica's faded blue eyes as

she clutched a fist to her well-endowed bosom. "Your father will be so disappointed."

Maggie placed a comforting arm around her aunt's soft shoulders. "Daddy's been dead for a year."

"He's up there watching over you." Jessica reached into her white Sunday purse, pulling out a fresh lacy handkerchief to dab her eyes. "I know your father was just plain tickled you were marrying Griff. He loved you both so much."

Maggie didn't want to think about her father and any personal feeling he might have had about such a union. "If anyone would have understood a police sting operation, it was BJ Bennington."

Wylie joined their small circle. "The department will reimburse you for your plane expenses, Jessica," he said, seemingly unaware that he had just dealt a deathblow to Jessica's dreams.

She rose to her feet, wrath sparking fury in her gaze. "Your precious department can keep its blood money, Sergeant." Maggie's aunt pointed an accusing, quivering finger at him. "Do you think money will make up for the fact that this wedding was a fake? That you tampered with something sacred and made it into a farce? Or that my Maggie and Griff won't make babies that I can spoil? I'm not getting any younger. I deserve to have a grandbaby to spoil just like everyone else."

Maggie had to bite her tongue. She wasn't going to get into a verbal duel and declare that Griff Murdock was the last person in the world she'd make a baby with.

From the corner of her eye, she could see Griff struggling to contain his amusement. She ignored him.

"Do you want me to have someone take you home, Aunt Jess?"

Her relative lifted her stout chin and gathered herself together. "I'll have Christine take me over to Selma Ritter's. Selma invited me to a bridge game tonight. I need to take my mind off this."

Jessica refused to look Maggie in the eye as she turned and stalked across the room.

As soon as Jessica was safely out of hearing range, Wylie lowered his voice and said, "I'm sorry if we got you in a tangle with your family, Maggie."

A wave of fatigue crashed over Maggie. "It's no more than I expected." There was no reason to point out this wasn't the first time she'd disappointed a member of her family. No doubt it wouldn't be the last. *That* realization made her even more tired.

"Of course if you want to put a smile on her face, there's nothing to stop you two from signing that marriage license the preacher is totin' around."

"Being part of one sting today is all I can handle," Maggie responded dryly.

Wylie loosened his tie with a wry glance at Griff. "Ouch. I think you've been stung, Griff. You need to work on your technique with women."

Griff appeared to take this under consideration. "Maybe Maggie could give me pointers."

"I don't have the patience or energy," Maggie said coolly. "Besides, that isn't part of the job I was hired for."

Griff grimaced. "I guess I'll be spending my wedding night alone."

Maggie knew he was kidding, but she couldn't stop a quiver rushing through her as she thought about what it would be like to actually be Griff's bride.

Wylie stuffed his tie into his pocket. "If I can't twist your arms any longer, I'd better get down to the station and put this case to bed."

After he left, Griff pulled his keys from his pocket and eyed Maggie. "Do you want a ride or would you prefer hiking a mile home in those high-heeled shoes?"

Her feet refused to be martyrs for the sake of avoiding any more contact with Griff. Besides, now that the case was over, she could afford to be magnanimous. With luck, she'd never have to see him again. She could get back to her life. "Where's your car?"

"Out front. We'll need to go upstairs and pick up whatever the thieves didn't take. Wylie said they left our stuff sitting in the front pews." As he reached over and opened the basement door for her, Maggie caught a whiff of his male scent. Her stomach clenched.

Breathe, Maggie, she ordered herself. She was almost out of this.

Without replying, Maggie led the way up the steps, all too conscious of Griff being just a step or two behind her.

They found most of their items still there.

Sifting through her bag, Maggie discovered the wallet she'd placed inside her purse gone. It was an old wallet she didn't use anymore, and she'd left a couple of dollars plus an expired credit card inside as bait. Grabbing her hangers and the clothes she'd worn to the church, she waited while Griff hefted a duffel bag that was sitting at the end of the pew.

With his back to her, she noticed how well the tux fit his body. The crisp black pants and the tailored jacket molded to his athletic body. She wondered how many female cops had wished they'd been the ones walking down the aisle with him, even for a phony ceremony. His sense of duty and unwavering commitment to the job could make an innocent woman believe he would be a devoted lover or spouse. What they didn't know was that devotion belonged to the job. No woman could ever compete.

Griff caught her watching him. "See something you like?"

She'd been around cops too many years to be embarrassed by blunt talk. "I need to get home and pack."

He twirled the key chain around his index finger, making no move toward the door. "Why did you agree to come back to the department and take this job?"

"For Wylie. He asked me to come back and work for the department. I could afford to postpone my plans for a few months, and I said yes." She rubbed the stiffness from her neck, rolling her shoulders in order to ease the tension that had been sitting there the entire afternoon.

"That's it?" A cynical twist lifted the edge of his mouth. "If memory serves me, your father asked you not to leave Pendleton but you did anyway."

Maggie froze. "Is that what you think?"

"After you left Pendleton, something in your dad died. He changed. He had no life."

She straightened as if slapped. "My father knew exactly why I left Pendleton and the department."

"You're a coward, Maggie. You ran."

She tried to pull off the veil atop her head but the pins refused to yield. "You don't know what you're talking about."

"Don't I?"

She lowered her hands from her head and clenched her fingers to keep from going at Griff's throat. "Did you ever stop to think that my father arranged for me to leave the department? That my very presence made him uncomfortable?"

Griff stood still. She could see him searching her face to see if she was telling the truth.

"You don't believe me?" she asked with mocking coldness. "Ask Wylie who handed in my resignation. They both wanted me to leave. Dad even arranged for me to get the deputy's job in Somerstown."

"Why?"

"That's none of your business." Her fingers coiled into a fist. "You might have been an authority on my father, but you don't know me, Murdock. You never did, and you never will. Now, if you're finished with your interrogation, I'd like a ride home. If you can't, I'll find someone else who will."

Griff had been a thorn in her side for too long. He'd been her father's partner, best friend and surrogate son. So much of her youthful energy had been devoted to seeking what Griff had been given freely. How many of her actions had been determined by his unwelcome presence in her life?

For the first time in her life, she was destined to be free from the ghosts of the past. Her father was forever gone. And Griff Murdock had no power or place in her future. She intended to make sure of that.

For a moment Griff didn't move.

She saw his gaze slice to her mouth and linger there. She braced herself. It was all she could do not to moisten her lips with the tip of her tongue. She tried to swallow and discovered her throat too dry for the effort. She wondered if her feet were up to the walk home. Blisters might be well worth the price of escaping Griff's company.

He finally broke the silence between them. "Let's go."

Relief beckoned. Making an effort to dispel the tension still holding her backbone hostage, Maggie managed to walk past him without touching so much as a hair on the back of his hand. The only sound between them was the whoosh of her dress, as it swirled around her legs and brushed the carpet.

They moved down the long church aisle, together this time. A fitting ending for the wedding. Only she wasn't a blushing bride eager to start married life with the man at her side.

Griff stepped in front of her as they came through the foyer. He swung open the big door, maneuvering so she could get by him. After the somber dimness of the church, the blinding glow of the sinking autumn sun caught her full in the face. Unable to see the steps in front of her, she stopped, trying to get her orientation. Suddenly the wind caught hold of her veil. She jerked back to catch it.

Griff nearly bumped into her. "What the heck—"

Ping!

At first the sound didn't make sense as she snagged the veil and tried to hold it close to her. Then Griff yelled, "Get down!"

Ping!

A cry tore from her lips as Griff's body hit hers. She tumbled to the ground under his weight. "Get off me!" she yelled. Jumping her twice in one day was more than she could stand.

''Someone's shooting at us. Roll. Now!'' he ordered with the snap of a drill sergeant.

Griff's arms locked around her body, and they rolled back through the open doorway. She clung to his shoulders, her purse caught between them.

As soon as they cleared the door frame, Griff struggled to his feet and slammed the door shut. Clumsily, staggering over the weight and bulk of the dress, Maggie found her own balance.

Grabbing her purse, she started to reach for her gun, and then stopped. Her hand felt damp.

She looked down.

Blood covered her hand, her dress and the floor.

Chilled horror tore through her like an Arctic blast. *Oh my lord!* ''What—''

''Damn.'' Griff's hoarse curse was the only warning she had.

She turned just in time to see big, sturdy Griff Murdock collapse at her feet.

Chapter 3

"Hate hospitals."

Maggie barely heard Griff's words amid the urgent, strident instructions being exchanged between the paramedics and the hospital staff as they pushed his stretcher through the doors of the emergency room.

A woman in a white coat rushed forward to meet them. "Take him into the trauma room," she commanded as they moved down the hall. She was petite, but there was nothing small about her cool professionalism. Everyone marched to her tune with each order she snapped.

The all-too-familiar smells and noises assaulted Maggie's senses, and she found her footsteps slowing. Just being here made the hairs on her arms stand up straight. An age old sense of hopelessness reappeared as the antiseptic odor assaulted her nostrils. She hadn't been in a hospital since her father's death a year ago, and she had to struggle to contain a surge of nausea. This wasn't the same hospital where her father had spent the last day of his life, but it had the same look and feel.

Another set of doors loomed ahead. She tried to release Griff's hand, but he wouldn't allow her. Despite his pallor and silence, his grip remained strong.

"No drugs." His voice had lowered to a labored hoarseness.

She squeezed his fingers. "Don't talk. Save your strength."

Wylie arrived at Griff's side. "Hang in there, man."

"Did you get the shooter?" Griff rasped.

His face engraved with deep-set worry, the older man gripped Griff's shoulder reassuringly. "Not yet, but we will." Someone would pay—and would pay dearly. Wylie and everyone else in the department wouldn't let a crime against one of their own go unpunished.

They reached a pair of swinging doors.

A sturdily built, middle-aged woman blocked them, forcing Maggie to relinquish Griff's hand. "You can't come in here."

Wylie used his impressive height to try to intimidate the nurse. "The hell we can't. We're police officers."

The woman, whose name badge read Alice Miller, RN, refused to budge. "This is my jurisdiction, not yours."

Wylie hadn't reached his position of authority by

giving in. He gestured toward Maggie. "That man in there needs her. She's his wife."

"Good, then she can fill out the admission forms while we take care of her husband." Nurse Miller apparently had earned a few commendations of her own. "In the meantime, if you want this man to be treated as quickly as possible, you'll both stay out of our way. It's been a busy day around here, and I don't want my staff tripping over weepy spouses and jumpy cops with itchy trigger fingers."

"I don't care what you want. I want someone in there with him."

Her eyebrows drew together. Nurse Miller, who wasn't much shorter than Wylie's six-foot height and looked as solid as a line backer, glared at him. "Don't make me get mean, sonny."

To Wylie's credit, he didn't slap handcuffs on her, although for a moment Maggie wasn't sure what he'd do. Few dared to challenge Wylie. And Maggie doubted he'd ever been called "sonny" in his life. He glared back. "Who's your best surgeon?"

"Dr. Anderson."

"Get him."

"That might be a bit tough. *She's* in Vegas at a doctor's convention." Nurse Miller didn't bat an eye or seem impressed by Wylie's steely attempt to take command. "I don't think this man can wait, unless you're more interested in collecting his death benefits than saving his life."

Wylie's nostril flared. "Who is your superior?"

She folded her arms across her ample chest.

''God.'' she replied, managing to stretch the name of the higher authority into two syllables.

Maggie might have enjoyed their repartee any other time or place if she hadn't seen Griff's color go from ash gray to a sickly white. The power play between Wylie and the nurse was costing precious time. Stepping between them, Maggie addressed the nurse. ''We want to consult with the doctor before any critical decisions are made. Your patient took a bullet in the leg and one in the shoulder.''

Nurse Miller gave Maggie's torn, bloodied wedding attire a quick sweep before pivoting away.

As the doors swished shut behind her, Wylie swore. ''I'll bet that woman worked for the KGB.'' He thrust agitated fingers through his hair, disturbing the silvery wave. ''No wonder people die in here.''

''Stop talking like that.'' Maggie wrapped her numb hands around her midsection. Her fingers still tingled from the tight grip Griff had had on her hand. The rest of her body and mind seemed numb, unable to fathom the notion of the stalwart Griff Murdock being felled by a bullet. ''He isn't going to die,'' she said, rubbing her hands up and down her arms.

The crevices on Wylie's weathered face deepened. He walked over to the doors and tried to peer through the frosted glass. ''You should be in there.''

''They can't do anything without our permission.''

He made a rude snort. ''They make their own rules. It must be something with the color of the walls or the ugly uniforms. Everyone I've ever cared about has come out in a zipped bag.''

Her patience snapped. "Stop it! Griff isn't going to die."

Wylie seemed as surprised as she was by her testiness. He gave her a cool assessing look and then attempted to smooth down the peaks of silvery hair he'd disturbed a moment earlier. "I need to find a phone. Let me know if anything changes."

Without waiting for her response, Wylie strode down the hall, leaving her alone in the pale corridor.

Maggie paced back and forth, still rubbing her arms, trying to ward off the eerie chill that built gooseflesh across her body.

She hated hospitals. Most cops did. Hospitals and their inmates were an alien world to be avoided at all costs. Cops understood the role and makeup of almost every player in society. They knew the talk and walked the walk alongside battered wives, abandoned children, drug pushers, white collar criminals and serial killers. Being an amateur psychologist went hand in hand with the job. Their knowledge gave them authority—until they stepped inside the antiseptic world of a hospital. Then they discovered how little they knew and what little authority they had when it came to determining the final battle between life and death. Unfortunately, too many lost the final battle. Just like her father had.

Perhaps that's why she knew she could no longer be a cop. She didn't believe in the invincibility of the job.

Wylie had asked her to reconsider leaving Pendleton, wanting to extend her contract. But Maggie didn't have energy for this kind of work any longer. She had to find a new life.

She stared at the frosty windowed doors and wondered how Griff was doing and then berated herself for caring. Murdock was a cop through and through. He'd live and die according to his job. Why should she worry about what was inevitable?

Wylie had insisted they take him to the city hospital instead of the nearby community facility close to the Wisconsin-Illinois border. During the endless ride to the general hospital in Pendleton, Griff hadn't said a word, his eyes opening and closing at random intervals. She didn't think she'd ever seen so much blood in her entire life.

The sight of him on the ground, blood pouring from his leg and shoulder wounds, had momentarily paralyzed her. For half a heartbeat, she'd gone blank as fear threatened to destroy what little composure she had left. Then reason reasserted itself. She refused to let him die. She vaguely recalled grabbing the hem of her wedding dress and ripping off a piece to staunch the flow of blood.

Griff's inner toughness had kept him conscious. If it hadn't been for the hard set to his mouth and the tight grip on her fingers, she might have believed he didn't feel any pain. But she knew his iron will was the only thing that kept him mute or from falling into unconsciousness.

She had to believe his alertness was a good sign.

The tightness of her wedding dress made her peruse the battered garment she still wore. It looked like the department would have to fork over the full price of

the dress. Most of the wedding props had been rented
from a shop on the east side of Pendleton. She doubted
if they'd take this dress back now.

Reaching up, Maggie tugged the pins out of her hair
one by one, freeing the mammoth weight of hair and
the veil. She wished she'd gone ahead and changed
before they'd tried to leave the church. There had been
a pair of slacks and a blouse in her bag. Would that
brief interruption of their departure made a difference
in stopping the shooting?

The past several months had been surreal after Wylie had called and asked her to rejoin the department.
At first she'd been reluctant, but she owed Wylie. And
she knew it would have pleased her father.

How ironic that she still wanted his approval, even
though he had been gone for more than a year.

She agreed to a six-month contract.

It had been three years since she'd left Pendleton
and the department. Working with the Pendleton officers again hadn't been nearly as uncomfortable as
she'd feared. But the engagement for the sting operation had been weird. She didn't enjoy being in the
spotlight, with everyone hovering around her plying
her with best wishes and hearty congratulations. Sales-
clerks had besieged her as she'd shopped for her wedding finery and registered for china. Misty-eyed little
old ladies had clucked their delight and regaled her
with romantic memories. Single women had treated
her like crowned royalty, hovering close, hoping to
absorb some of the limelight. The strangeness had
been uncomfortable for the only child of a cop who
sometimes forgot to come home on Christmas Day.

The worst had been listening to the crowing enthusiasm of her fellow officers. Who would have thought a group of policemen could get so excited about a wedding? But they had. Closer than any tight-knit family, the Pendleton Police Department had never planned a wedding before. From the wedding cake to the marriage license to the limo service, there wasn't a detail that hadn't been subjected to dissection, lengthy discussions and raunchy humor. Nothing had been private or sacred. They openly speculated about Griff's and Maggie's sex life, where they'd live, what kind of house they should buy and how many children they'd have.

Maggie had endured their incessant ribbing with gritted teeth. She understood that so many aspects of their jobs as police officers in the south central Wisconsin community of seventy thousand bore the grim reality of the ugliness gaining a strong foothold in their fair city. Only a week ago, a man had killed his female roommate when he discovered her sleeping with another man. Even though he'd never dated this woman, he claimed to love her and couldn't bear to see her with anyone else.

A crime of passion.

Love and hate. So closely intertwined. Each one capable of incredible pain and destruction.

The sound of footsteps clipping against the tile floor brought a surge of relief as Wylie rounded the corner and strode toward her. His frown hadn't lessened.

She met him halfway. "Have they found anything?"

The rigid roads of tension lining his face foretold his answer. "They're working on it."

She pressed fingers against her suddenly aching forehead. "Did the shooter think we'd release the church robbers if he brought down a cop?"

"Maybe it wasn't the church robbers who were after him."

She stopped massaging her temples. "Who else could it have been?"

Wylie dug into his pocket and produced the small dog-eared note pad that he always carried with him. "That's what we need to find out. Guy Fergus has been released."

The name sounded vaguely familiar. "The man who set fire to his own house, killing his wife and two daughters? I thought he was a lifer with no parole."

"Apparently Fergus brushed his teeth enough times a day to warrant a release on good behavior." Wylie's frustration echoed a tired theme of a familiar song. New lyrics to an old tune.

"Damn."

"Right." He lowered his voice as a woman and her young son walked by and went into a nearby waiting room.

Maggie turned her back on them so her words wouldn't carry. "Is Fergus being brought in for questioning?"

"They're looking for him. But the shooter could have been anyone who had a grudge against either you or Griff."

"Me?" Then she frowned as the memory of the wind catching her veil flashed through Maggie's mind.

She lifted the frilly garment in her hand and looked for the evidence she didn't want to find. When she found it, she froze.

Before she could say anything, Wylie plucked the veil from her hand. "Where did this hole come from?"

Maggie shook her head. That moment in time seemed to grow bigger with each passing second. She didn't want to believe Griff took a bullet meant for her. "I wasn't the one who was shot."

Wylie's gaze was direct and piercing. "Who says the shooter wasn't a bad shot? You were both standing in front of the church. Griff wasn't necessarily the target. Or maybe both of you were."

The laughter that spurted from her mouth contained no humor. "That doesn't make any sense."

"It does if someone wanted to stop you two from getting married."

"I've only been living in Pendleton for the past few months. Why would anyone try to kill me?"

"You worked in the department until three years ago. Maybe someone has been biding his time, waiting for you to return."

Maggie shivered. The hallway seemed almost cave-like, cutting off light from the real world outside. "What's the next step?"

Before he could answer, the double doors opened from the outside and Maggie's Aunt Jessica stepped through them. She wasn't alone. At her side was Reverend Foxworth.

Her aunt started speaking before she was a half-dozen yards away. "We got here as soon as we could."

Maggie stiffened at the sight of the black book in the reverend's hands. "Griff doesn't need last rites. He isn't going to die."

"Of course he's not, dear. But neither should he go into surgery without a loving wife at his side," Aunt Jessica stated firmly.

Out of the corner of her eye, Maggie saw Wylie struggle to contain a smile as they both realized her aunt hadn't given up her quest to get her niece married off even if the groom was semiconscious. Knowing she wasn't going to get any help from Wylie, Maggie managed to hang on to her patience. "Griff and I don't want to get married."

"Nonsense, girl. You two were made for each other. Anyone can see you two are perfect—"

"Griff's unconscious," Maggie interrupted with a lie, unwilling to stand here and argue.

Her aunt's hands flew to her mouth, her eyes watering. "Oh that poor, poor boy."

The reverend slipped his little black book into his pocket. "Since I can't marry you two, why don't I offer a prayer for your husband's...I mean, Mr. Murdock's recovery. Would that be okay?"

Maggie smiled her relief. "That would be great. We'd appreciate—"

"No, we wouldn't," Wylie interrupted.

Maggie swung toward him with surprise. "I don't think Griff would object to a prayer."

He waved her question away with impatience. "That's not what I meant. The prayer is fine, but I think the reverend here should finish marrying you two.''

"Forget it,'' Maggie said flatly.

"I thought Griff was unconscious.'' Jessica's expression altered between hope and suspicion.

"I'm sure he's conscious by now,'' Wylie assured her.

Maggie squeezed Wylie's arm. "Could I talk to you privately?'' Her pressure didn't seem to phase him.

In fact, he didn't even seem to notice it. "I want the guy who did this.''

"So do I.'' Maggie wished her aunt wasn't standing at her elbow.

"We don't know why this guy winged Griff. Anything is possible.''

"The thieves—''

"Might or might not be responsible. We have no evidence so far that there was a third thief,'' he said. "There's also the possibility this shooting might have occurred because someone believed you two were actually going to be man and wife.''

"That's ridiculous.'' She fingered the tightening collar of the wedding dress, trying to find a bit of breathing room. Now she wished she had chosen a dress with a lower neckline that allowed more air to flow over her heated skin. The hospital corridor was becoming decidedly stuffy. "The gunman was probably the thieves' lookout man, and when things went bad, he wanted to get even and tried to take out Griff.''

Wylie waved her damaged veil in front of her, a movement sharp with impatience. "It doesn't track. A smart thief would keep his head low. Trying to kill either of you would finger his presence, ensuring we'd come looking. He'd want us to think there were only two people involved.''

''Who said he was smart?''

''He's smart enough to pull off a shooting under our noses.'' When she didn't comment, he lowered his voice to a personal level. ''Think about it, Maggie. Why would a thief, who will probably get off with a slap on the wrist or get out of prison early on good behavior, risk a life sentence?''

His reasoning made her nervous. ''What about the woman they beat up at the last wedding?''

''A good lawyer could get the charges diminished or dropped during a plea bargain. Either way, he won't get much of a sentence,'' he said patiently as he shredded another one of her arguments.

She hated his logic. But she couldn't argue against it, either. They could create a lot of possibilities for why the shooting occurred, but until they caught the gunman, all their theories were suppositions. Nothing more. She sighed. ''So you want us to pretend to be married?''

''Not pretend. I want it on record so there's no doubt in anyone's mind that the deed is done.'' The granite edge in his tone bespoke his determination. ''We make this marriage official so whoever pointed a gun at you *knows* you're actually married.''

Shock raced through her with the devastating impact of a lightning bolt. ''You're joking.''

''You don't have to sleep with Griff. Just see through this whole charade. You can annul the marriage as soon as we've caught this guy and Griff's back on his feet.''

"Or you might decide it's best to stay married," Aunt Jessica inserted hopefully.

The air in the hallway became thinner, harder to draw into Maggie's lungs. ''In case you've forgotten, this wasn't a real wedding. What if someone finds out the truth?''

Wylie gave her a look that had made more than one prisoner squirm. ''We did everything to make it look real. Very few people knew the whole truth. Only those assigned to this case were alerted in the department. No memos were circulated stating otherwise. That ceremony was real except for your signatures penned to the dotted line.''

Her aunt and the reverend didn't interrupt but Maggie felt the pressure of their presence.

She tried to think but couldn't. She took a step out of their tight little circle and stared at the door that separated them from Griff. ''The thieves must have had a lookout man stationed nearby,'' she thought aloud, trying to rationalize her favored theory—the only theory worth considering for the sake of her sanity. ''It's the only thing that makes sense.''

"Then why wait to shoot at you and Griff after we'd taken away the suspects?'' Wylie's tone was smooth, as if he knew he had her in the palm of his hand. He splayed his hands. ''Why not gun down the arresting officers and try to spring his associates?''

She hated his reasoning, hated even more the idea of tying herself legally to Griff. ''It could be one of Griff's enemies. He's made more than a few.''

"Or it could be one of yours. You put away your share before you left Pendleton. We all make enemies in this business.'' Placing his hands on her shoulders, he didn't cut her any slack or allow her to dodge the blunt reality. "You don't have to like it. You just have to follow through with the operation until it's finished. Covering all our bases is the best chance we've got of nailing this guy. We have to assume he wanted either one or both of you dead and presume he'll try to make another attempt. He'll come looking."

"We'll be targets."

"You'll be protected. Think of it as an undercover job."

"And if we don't continue this charade?"

"We'll lose a potential cop killer. He'll go into hiding and resurface again when one or both of you least expects it. You could be sitting ducks. Do you want to keep looking over your shoulder the rest of your life?"

Maggie didn't believe she was a target. And yet, if she hadn't stepped back at that last minute....

Had Griff taken a bullet meant for her?

Her wedding dress wasn't any protection against the icy fear stealing along her backbone.

Wylie tightened his hands on her shoulders. "Make those marriage vows legal, so we can find this guy."

"For how long?" She knew the answer even before she asked the question.

"As long as it takes. We protect our own, and we'll go the extra mile to bring in this guy, lock him up and throw away the key." He relaxed his fingers and gave her a crooked grin. "It's not like either of you has a beau or girlfriend that you have to make excuses to.''

The walls loomed closer. She made one more stab to push them back. "What makes you think Griff will even agree to the marriage?"

"He's a cop. He'll do whatever it takes to bring in his man. You, more than anyone else, should know that.''

She did know it.

Griff Murdock was first and foremost a cop—just like her father. But as much as she respected the code and commitment they lived by, she'd vowed never to marry one. And she'd certainly never marry Griff Murdock, the man who had always been between her and her father's undivided attention.

Griff could put the kibosh to this crazy plan, and she'd have a chance of escaping. But she knew he wouldn't.

She also knew that if she'd been the one who had been hit at the church, Griff wouldn't be standing in the hall dithering while her life hung on the line. He'd already have his name on the dotted line and be ordering the hospital staff to get her into surgery stat.

Slumping against the wall, Maggie blew at the piece of scraggly hair that had once been a part of her fancy hairdo. This morning when she'd had it done at one of the local beauty salons seemed so long ago. "You have all the answers, don't you?"

"If I did, Griff wouldn't have two bullets in him and you wouldn't be standing here right now." She heard the pain of self-blame in his tone before he tucked the wayward strand of hair behind her ear and brushed a rough knuckle against her cheek. "I don't want anything to happen to either of you. What's it going to be?"

Maggie looked past his shoulder at Aunt Jessica, who was looking anxious. Wylie was right. She didn't want to keep looking over her shoulder. Nor did she want anyone to get caught in the cross fire again if she was the intended target.

She finally gave in and jerked her head in agreement, before reminding him, "I've got to leave by the end of the week to get back to Somerstown. I want to open my store in three weeks."

"We can work around that." Wylie's promise came quickly before she could retract her agreement. "I'll go talk to that battle-ax of a nurse and ask if we can see Griff."

As he disappeared into the next room, Jessica came over to her side and patted her hand. "You're doing the right thing, honey."

Maggie nodded, wishing she had her aunt's confidence.

Seconds later Wylie reappeared. "We need to make this fast, Reverend. They want to get Griff ready for surgery."

As soon as they entered the room, two nurses and a resident moved aside. Griff's eyes were closed. The reverend went immediately to Griff's side and touched his arm. "How are you doing, Mr. Murdock?"

Griff grunted. His eyes cracked open to a slit.

"There's no time for chitchat, Reverend," Wylie said tersely. "You got that marriage license?"

"It just needs to be signed. I bent the rules and had

the witnesses sign their names already.'' He pulled a paper from his Bible and offered a pen to Griff. ''Do you think you can sign this?''

Griff's eyes opened again. Ignoring the paper in front of him, his gaze cleared and settled on Maggie. ''You won't take advantage of me, will you, Bennington?''

His humor helped solidify her courage. She took her position next to him. ''With two bullet holes in you, you're safe. I only take advantage of men who can go the distance.''

The corner of his mouth twitched. ''Hand me the pen, Rev.''

With a bit of maneuvering, Griff scrawled his name across the documents. Then it was Maggie's turn.

The deed was done and over within seconds.

Reverend Foxworth pocketed the papers. Straightening, he gave them a wry grin. ''We've done things a bit backward but it's now official in the eyes of the Lord and the law.''

Nurse Miller attempted to reclaim her post next to Griff. ''Okay, people, move aside. We need to get him into surgery before that fracture sets.''

Aunt Jessica placed her body between Griff and the nurse. ''They haven't kissed yet.''

''Aunt Jessica—''

''Perhaps we should have a prayer instead,'' the Reverend interrupted.

But her aunt refused to give in. ''Maggie, quit being such a ninny and kiss Griff so they can patch him up. Do you want the poor man to die without having kissed his bride?''

"But I—"

"Oh for crying out loud, kiss him, girl," Wylie ordered, "and we can all get out of here."

Aware of everyone watching her, Maggie tried to pretend the man in front of her was no different than anyone else she might kiss. With any luck, and considering all the pain he was in, he'd never even remember.

His closed eyelids gave her hope. Not giving herself any time to think, she leaned forward and brushed her lips quickly against his. The coldness of his mouth shocked her. She started to move back when his eyelids opened slightly. His lips moved, and she had to bend close to him to hear him.

"What did you say?" she asked.

"You need practice…. We'll work on it later."

Before she could retort to his outrageous statement, Nurse Miller shooed them away from her patient.

After their abrupt escort from the room, Jessica dragged one of her handkerchiefs from her handbag and blotted the wetness from the corner of her eyes. "Oh, that was truly lovely. Just like when my Harold kissed me on our wedding day." She delicately dabbed once again and then beamed at Maggie. "I know your father is smiling from heaven. You've made him so happy, my dear."

Maggie was glad this farce made someone happy. She, on the other hand, longed to grab one of those lacy hankies from her aunt's purse and bawl her eyes out.

Chapter 4

"Why did you agree to sign the marriage certificate?"

Griff's question three days after their so-called wedding caught Maggie by surprise.

"Why wouldn't I?"

"You wanted to run. Admit it," he prodded her.

Maggie had to bite her lip to keep from putting him in his place.

Ever since they'd moved Griff into a private room an hour and a half after he'd emerged from surgery, he'd said little. The pain medication he'd reluctantly agreed to take had made him groggy and disinclined to talk.

They had removed two bullets from him. One had chewed a hole through his thigh, producing a gusher when it punctured a major blood vessel. The other had broken the clavicle bone in his shoulder before it ended up lodged perilously close to his heart. Screws had been inserted to hold the bone in place while it healed. Although his surgery had taken almost four hours—considerably longer than expected—during the past twenty-four hours, Griff had made significant progress. The doctor predicted he should make a complete recovery.

Maggie eyed Griff's expressionless face, trying to determine his mood. In a shapeless hospital gown, his dark hair mussed, Griff appeared remote, his face creased in stoic ridges. He had declined the last dose of pain medicine, and she couldn't imagine how he bore the discomfort or the trauma of the past few days.

Everything seemed to be a blur.

Noticing his intent gaze, she realized he was waiting for an answer. "If you die, I'll be your next of kin. That's why I agreed to marry you."

Griff produced a rude sound. "You never did lie very well."

"Who says I'm lying? How much would I have gotten if you had kicked the bucket?"

"Not a windfall, if that's what you're hoping for. We both know cops don't make any money."

"They also make lousy spouses," Maggie replied coolly, pretending to examine her nails.

Griff turned his head and stared up at the ceiling. He couldn't argue with her. They were especially lousy when they were immobilized and unable to relieve themselves without calling for help.

He hated the helplessness, the lack of control. Growing up as a ward of the state, he'd always taken care of himself. What choice had he had? Looking back, he was damned glad for it. He'd learned to be independent, not to count on what he couldn't provide for himself. Part of his decision to become a police officer was his overwhelming need to stay in control and to take charge of any situation. Yet with his right leg immobilized in a cast and his left arm stuck in a sling, he was as helpless as a newborn babe.

Forcing his mind off his own disgusting weakness, he squinted at Maggie, who was pacing around the room. She and Wylie had taken turns staying with him ever since he'd been wheeled out of recovery. Maggie had been here the most. That surprised him even if she was now his wife on paper.

His wife.

Hell, he must have been sicker than he thought. He'd always known if by the remotest chance he was ever so stupid as to get married again, he'd choose a woman who didn't have too many expectations of him, had a pleasant, quiet disposition and would put up with his being a cop. Maggie Bennington flunked on all accounts. She was even flightier than his late wife had been.

Of course, he knew he wouldn't be Maggie's idea of Prince Charming, either.

He wondered what Wylie had done to coerce her into signing that marriage certificate. They had always struck sparks off each other—sparks of animosity mostly. But a different kind of fireworks erupted within him the minute he'd spotted Maggie at the other end of the wedding aisle. He hadn't been able to take his eyes off her or squelch the seductive heat spreading through his loins.

Maggie had always done her best to be one of the guys. She'd downplayed her femininity, hiding her curves under the formality of her uniform or a pair of jeans overlapped by long-tailed shirts. But she hadn't been able to hide her female assets beneath that wedding dress. Every part of her breathed femininity.

And there hadn't been a part of his body that hadn't noticed.

Standing uncomfortably close to her during the church service, her scent teased and fanned the raw want within him, intensifying his desire to an unbearable level. He'd wanted to kiss that frozen snootiness off her face and change it into something real and wanton.

And that's exactly what he had been thinking about when he walked out that church door and into the path of a gunman's bullet.

He couldn't believe lust for a woman had overridden his sixth sense. He'd always been able to smell trouble. It was a sense he'd developed and learned to listen to over the years.

So what had happened? Why hadn't that uneasiness clawing inside his gut sent him on alert?

Because Maggie Bennington had donned a wedding dress?

On some level, he'd always known that Maggie was a dangerous woman. She tried to put on a façade of toughness, but she was too soft for the job. Once he'd witnessed her giving her lunch to a smart-mouthed juvenile who had been caught stealing a pizza from a delivery man. Another time, she had taken several small children home with her so they could wait for their father instead of being turned over to Social Services. And ever since Maggie had been back in Pendleton, she spent several hours each week at a shelter, working with the kids.

Was Griff now one her charity cases? Was that why she was still hanging around?

Maggie had deserted her father when he'd needed her most. And then BJ died. Griff couldn't forget that. But Maggie had insisted BJ had arranged for her to leave. Had he? Why?

Griff's inner turmoil came to an abrupt end as Maggie suddenly stopped pacing and swung around to look at him. "Why did you agree to this arrangement?" she asked.

Griff noticed how she had avoided referring to the arrangement as a marriage. He considered her tight face and the shadows lurking in the back of her eyes. Those shadows had been there ever since he'd met her twelve years ago. She'd been fourteen and he'd been twenty-two. She'd never made it any secret that he was one shadow she didn't need and wanted to be rid of. He thought that's what he wanted, too.

But the image of her rushing to his side after he was shot rose to the forefront of his mind. He remembered too clearly the tension on her face as she'd taken charge while trying to stem the flow of blood with a piece torn from her white wedding gown. She'd muttered nonsensical stuff, blathering on in a soothing, unhurried voice meant to reassure him that his wounds were minor. Yet in the green mirrors of her eyes, he saw the truth, realizing the pressure she exerted was keeping him from floating downstream in his own blood.

He kept conscious by focusing on her, living for the sound of her voice. For a man who'd lived most of his life on the outside looking in, each word, each gesture had imprinted itself in his head, replaying over and over again.

Every time he closed his eyes, he saw her face during the long, painful ride in the ambulance to the hospital and how she'd maintained a tight hold on his hand. Or had he gripped hers? He decided it didn't matter. She hadn't pulled away. She'd just been there. He had seen little softness in his life and couldn't help lapping it up like a starving hound.

Why had she bothered?

Why did he care? He usually hated that kind of dependency.

From the closed expression on Maggie's face, Griff figured she was mentally bracing herself for his answer.

He turned away and retreated to staring up at the ceiling again. Neither of them needed an extra complication right now. It was better to play it safe and stick to the rules they'd both followed since BJ's death. "It seemed like the thing to do," he finally answered.

Her posture relaxed a bit. Pointing to his water pitcher, she asked, "Do you want me to have the nurse refill that?"

They both knew he only had to push a button to get anything he needed. He let her go. "Sure."

After he heard the door shut behind her, he tried to

sort through what had happened and the implications. Why had she worked so hard to save his life? She could have left his side after they tucked him into the ambulance. It certainly would have made sense.

His partner's daughter had resented him since the day BJ had brought Griff home and introduced them. She couldn't hide her animosity anymore than she could stop trying to fix a young punk's problems. For the most part, Griff considered her a pain in the rear end and had done his best to ignore her.

Not even after BJ had died and they'd gone through this engagement charade had she changed her opinion of him. And Griff never tried to dissuade it.

What would have happened if he had?

She'd even shown up at the wedding wearing something a nun would wear. The minute he caught sight of that damnable mummy dress, he'd known she'd chosen it to provoke him. What she hadn't realized was how he had fantasized through most of the ceremony about releasing each one of those tiny pearl buttons, one button at a time, and slowly removing the dress from her body.

Their physical contact when he'd thrown his body over hers to protect her had only given color to his more vivid fantasies. He'd learned Maggie's curves were in all the right places. She had breasts that begged to be touched. A lush, sensuous mouth that tormented a man to lose his head and take full advantage of the invitation she unconsciously offered. Velvety green eyes that had the power to seduce a saint.

And he was certainly no saint.

He'd wanted her. Even in this sterile hospital bed, he wanted a woman he could never have.

The sound of the door opening, brought Griff back to the present as temptation returned. Every fiber of him responded to Maggie's reappearance. Griff could easily discern things he tried to keep from noticing. The sexiness of her walk. Her scent. The twitch and sway of her hips.

She wore a denim long-tailed shirt over faded jeans. A unisex ensemble. The attire would have been successful camouflage before the wedding. But not anymore. He remembered having her sweet body twitch and thrash under his as if it were only ten minutes ago. Recalling her softness and the enticing view of bare thigh made the stabbing throbs in his shoulder and leg insignificant.

Who would have thought BJ Bennington's daughter would grow into a siren? The way her body had cradled against Griff's was proving hard to forget. He wanted nothing more than to bury his fingers into her shoulder-length, untamed hair that was a shade riper than auburn, cup her face and finish the kiss they'd started in the emergency room. It was all he could think about as he'd hovered at the brink of unconsciousness. Thinking of sex had helped him hang on to his wits. Now, it was driving him crazy. He wondered how many stitches he'd pop if he rose from this bed, picked her up in his arms and made love to her right now.

Two bullet holes in his body were probably less life threatening than tangling with one Maggie Bennington. He would do well to keep that in mind.

Only he couldn't forget she'd saved his life. There was an obligation there if nothing else.

She set the pitcher of water on the tray in front of him. "Anything else you need?" she asked.

"Do you have a list of wifely duties I can choose from?" The wound in his thigh started to prickle and pain, but he ruthlessly ignored it by directing his full concentration and frustration on Maggie.

Her gaze narrowed. "Don't push your luck, Murdock." Her color was high despite her dampening tone.

It gave him some satisfaction to know he wasn't the only one affected by the sexual currents zipping between them.

She picked up a magazine and pretended to read. That suited Griff just fine as he indulged in the pleasure of watching her, noticing the rosy hue to her cheeks, which made a lie out of her supposed disinterest.

Most redheads tended to look blotchy whenever a flush oozed across their skin. But Maggie had smooth satiny skin. When rosy and bothered....

Suddenly Griff realized Maggie was giving him a frosty expression from her side of the room. Had she guessed his thoughts? No. She would go straight for his throat if she could guess.

He couldn't resist prodding her. "How much longer are you going to hang around here?"

"If you hadn't gotten yourself shot, I'd be gone by now. I've got to get back to my job."

"You were a cop in Somerstown?" he asked.

"Are you interrogating me?"

''You have something else you'd rather talk about?''

Her gaze lowered to her clenched hands. ''The Somerstown Police Department was short-staffed. I worked two years for them.''

''Are you going back to rejoin them?''

She shook her head and settled back into her chair, appearing more relaxed than she had when she'd returned to the room. ''No, I'm buying a gift shop.''

Griff's lip curled. ''You're going to give up trying to save the world from a herd of messed-up kids?''

She lifted her chin. ''There's other ways to help. Not every problem can be solved carrying a gun.''

''Tell that to the kids who are better armed than the police.''

''Maybe they don't have a choice.''

''Everyone has a choice, sweetheart,'' he drawled. He better than anyone knew that.

''I'm not your sweetheart!''

''A marriage license says you are.'' He shouldn't be baiting her, but he liked the green flames in her eyes a heck of a lot more than the frost.

Maggie rose to her feet, looking ready to throttle him, when Wylie sauntered into the room. The older man's frown changed to a grin as he correctly interpreted Maggie's militant stance and the waves of hostility darting between the two of them. ''Fighting already? Nothing I like to see more than a happily married couple.''

Maggie turned the full force of her glare on him. ''You're hardly an authority on happy marriages. Two wives divorced you, Wylie.''

"But I did love them." He gave her a roguish wink, a mocking gesture that couldn't quite hide his own pain. "If only they could have tolerated my demanding mistress."

She looked away. "We all know marrying a cop sports a high price tag." Griff noticed how she softened her words even though she couldn't quite take out the sting.

Wylie shrugged. "Sometimes it is and sometimes it isn't. It depends on the people involved." His gaze flickered from Maggie to Griff and then back again.

She wasn't going to argue the hazards of being married to a cop. The statistics spoke for themselves. She decided it was long past time to change the subject. "What happens after Griff is released from the hospital? I want to leave no later than Friday."

The troubled expression Wylie had been wearing when he walked into the room reappeared. He hooked a chair with his index finger and pulled it alongside the bed. "The suspects we've interrogated all have alibis. It's going to take a while to clear everyone. The shooter could be anyone."

"What about the guy who set fire to his own house, killing his wife and two daughters?" Griff asked.

"Guy Fergus is taking a vacation. He's a changed man—or so his attorney says."

Maggie walked over to the window. "That sounds flimsy."

"Yeah. So flimsy it's probably true."

She looked back at Wylie over her shoulder. "There weren't any other clues left at the scene?"

He scratched the back of his head. "We found a

rumpled copy of the wedding invitation across the street. Both of your names were circled several times like a bull's-eye target.''

"Any fingerprints?" Griff asked.

Wylie shook his head. "Not a one." Anyone who knew the older man well could see the fury he was trying to hold in check. "He must have worn gloves. That's what makes it even more suspicious. Everyone had to hand over an invitation to get inside the church."

"That's it?"

"The list of wedding guests has disappeared."

Maggie blinked. "Where was it?"

Wylie hesitated and then admitted, "In a file folder on my desk. It could have been misplaced."

"Or it might have been stolen."

An ominous silence hung in the room.

Griff leaned back into the pillows. The movement produced a sharp twinge in his shoulder, only bearable because of the tight lock he had on his jaw. "So it could have been another cop."

Wylie sighed. "There's any number of people who walk in and out of my office every day. It could have been anyone. Either way, this shooting looks premeditated." He motioned to Maggie. "Sit down, Maggie. Your hovering is making me nervous. We need to create a plan for the two of you."

"I'm not part of this. Griff is the one who got shot," Maggie said.

"That hole in your veil can't be ignored. He might have missed you and hit Griff instead. We don't know who the target was."

Griff could see how much Maggie wanted to argue. She reluctantly lowered herself into the chair.

Wylie retrieved his notebook from his pocket. Flipping it open, he studied several pages. "The reality is we've got a cop shooter at large. We don't know who it is, which one of you was meant to take that bullet or why." Closing the notebook, he tapped it against his hand. "We've got a couple of options. One, we could tuck you both away in a hotel room and assign round-the-clock guards."

Maggie shook her head almost vehemently. The idea of being shut up with Griff in a hotel room didn't bear consideration. "Count me out. If everything goes right, I want to open my store within the next month."

"I'm allergic to the stale air inside hotel rooms," Griff said flatly. "Let's hear Plan B."

Wylie pocketed his notebook. "You both can hide out in my cabin in Jonas Falls."

Before Griff could voice his objection, Maggie's chair crashed to the floor as she jumped to her feet. "No way," she said.

Wylie motioned her to sit down. "Hear me out."

She didn't return to her seat, but she pressed her lips into a tight line and folded her arms tightly across her chest.

"Griff, you'll be out of commission for a while and will need assistance getting around," Wylie said.

"I'm not completely helpless."

"No, if you were, I wouldn't even suggest that you leave the hospital. This isn't the perfect solution, but I know you're both too damn stubborn to go into protective custody. And I don't have the manpower to keep track of both of you. So, the next best thing is for you two to play out the marriage angle and go to the cabin. I'll be the only person who knows how to contact you. And when our guy comes sniffin' around, he'll have to come through me.''

Maggie's mouth dried. She paced back and forth. ''We can't even get along inside a hospital room. What makes you think we could get along locked up inside a cabin? There has to be another option.''

Griff didn't say anything. For once in his life, his brain seemed curiously void of any ideas, even though his fate rested on the outcome.

Wylie drummed his fingers against the arms of his chair. ''I don't have any other solutions short of locking you both in a jail cell to keep you out of harm's way. But then I'd worry about the well-being of my officers and the other prisoners.''

''I don't need a guard or a nursemaid,'' Griff stated with no emotion.

''Of course you do,'' Maggie said irritably. ''How are you going to get around with your leg in a cast and your arm in a sling?''

''I'll manage.''

His stubbornness irritated Maggie even more.

For a moment Wylie let the hostility simmer.

When the tension had dulled a bit, he leaned forward, planting his forearms atop his thighs. ''The way I see it, Jonas Falls is a good hundred and fifty miles from here. The tourists have all left for the season. It's quiet up there.''

The idea of spending weeks or months trapped inside a house with Griff made Maggie break into a cold sweat. They'd gotten through the past few weeks by being polite and professional. They had both been acting for the sake of the job. But living in the same house together…? She wasn't that good of an actor.

On the other hand, what choice did she have?

When neither man spoke, she swung around and caught the cryptic visual exchange between the two men.

A drape of remoteness closed Griff's expression, making it impossible to decipher. She expected him to object to this ridiculous scenario and when he didn't, she realized he was allowing her to make the decision. His choices were limited. Wherever he went, he'd need help. She could almost sympathize with him if he were anyone other than who he was.

Maggie was the one who had to make the decision.

It would be easy to leave town.

There was no one to make awkward explanations to. Aunt Jessica had already flown back to Florida so she could pack for a month long cruise she was taking with friends. Wylie could make explanations to their associates at the department.

Despite the logic, Maggie toyed with the idea of walking out the door and letting Wylie and Griff work out a different plan. One that wouldn't include her. No one would be surprised. Least of all Griff. He probably expected it. He'd always believed women didn't have staying power.

Maggie was tempted to prove him right.

Temptation wasn't enough, not after feeling the warmth of his blood seep through her fingers.

She had no choice—if for no other reason than

she'd feel guilty leaving him to fend on his own. Her
soft heart had always gotten her into trouble. Why
should now be any different? "All right, I'll do it—
just until Griff gets off his crutches."

Wylie moved to his feet quickly before she could
recant her decision. "Good. I'll make the arrangements."

He turned to replace his chair to its rightful place.

Behind his back, Griff's brooding gaze met Maggie's. Was he surprised she'd caved in? She kept her
own expression blank, hiding her feelings and motives, her teeth hurting from the lock she had on her
jaw.

It didn't matter what he thought or what he believed.

For better or worse, she had committed herself.

Chapter 5

Maggie slipped out the side door of the hospital. Tucking her head into her collar, she kept her face hidden.

A plain car pulled up next to the curb, and she slid into the passenger seat.

Christine drove the vehicle around the corner and cruised down the residential street before saying, "No tails, Maggie. It's all clear."

Maggie straightened and let out a deep sigh. She needed to get clothes from their respective apartments, and Wylie refused to let her go alone. "Thanks for picking me up."

Christine smiled, looking every bit the cop today. "This was easier than being your bridesmaid. At least I'm not handicapped with panty hose. Where shall I drop you first?"

"Take me to Griff's apartment."

Christine grinned. "Anxious to see how your new husband lives?"

"Something like that."

Christine had been Maggie's only confidante during the past few months. Dark-haired with a long leggy frame, Christine could have had any man in the department, but she turned down all of their offers.

"How's Griff doing?" Christine asked.

"About as well as you'd expect."

"Irritable as hell, is he?"

"In spades."

The tension started easing from Maggie's shoulders. She had no idea how she was going to handle the next six weeks of Griff's company. The very idea made her shoulder blades itch and the blood vessels along her forehead pound.

"The word is that you two are heading out of town for your honeymoon." The lightness of Christine's voice didn't mask the question.

Maggie wanted nothing more than to unload all her frustrations about this so-called marriage and what lay ahead. However, despite her complete trust in the other woman, she couldn't sacrifice the investigation or Griff's safety. A possible leak in the department hadn't been ruled out.

"It won't be much of a honeymoon with Griff's injuries."

Maggie was grateful when Christine didn't press her for more details. The other woman must have been curious about why Maggie had agreed to finalize the marriage vows. Christine knew as well as anyone that the last person on earth Maggie would have chosen to marry was Griff Murdock. And yet, Wylie had now spread the word that Maggie and Griff had signed the marriage papers, were legally wed and were preparing for their honeymoon.

Just the word "honeymoon" created a big knot inside Maggie. Only in the throes of a nightmare would she have dreamed of going on one with Griff.

Christine rechecked the rearview mirror before making a right hand turn. They clocked another few blocks before she pulled up in front of a white-fenced two-story house. "This is it. Do you want some help?"

Maggie shook her head. "I've got it covered. This shouldn't take long."

"I'll take a spin around the neighborhood and check out the area."

Maggie thrust open the car door and hurried up the sidewalk, fishing Griff's keys from her pocket. She'd never been to the boardinghouse before. Griff told her Mrs. Harris, the landlady, would be gone. This was the afternoon she visited an ailing relative in a nursing home on the other side of town.

Letting herself in the front door, Maggie didn't take time to look around. She crossed the floor and headed up the stairs. Fortunately she didn't meet any of the other tenants. Griff's room was the second one on the right. She fitted the key he'd given her into the lock.

Once inside she took a deep breath, trying to dispel the uneasiness that seemed to increase tenfold.

Her eyes took in the sparse furnishings, skipping hurriedly past the king-sized bed. It didn't surprise her that Griff's place would be neat. He carried an innate tidiness about him, which went along with his aura of remoteness. There was little to reveal the inner man, his goals, desires or passions.

Don't even think about it, Maggie. Just do what you have to do and get out of here.

She gave herself a mental slap and headed to the closet to find the suitcase she'd been told would be there. She flung the big bag on the bed and quickly emptied the drawers of their contents. She tried to keep her mind empty and not to give any weight to the realization that Griff was a boxers' man. After she emptied the bureau, she tackled the bathroom. She stowed his shaving gear in a separate bag along with the few other toiletries she'd been told to bring.

The impersonal environment made her even more nervous about the weeks ahead of her. It wouldn't have surprised her if he catalogued his medicine cabinet. Or labeled his socks.

What did she really know about Griff Murdock? He'd been her father's partner. So what? That didn't tell her what he'd be like to live with.

What possible landmines did she have the potential of tripping?

Behave, Maggie. Next you'll be speculating if he sleeps on the left side or the right? Touching his clothes made everything seem too familiar for her peace of mind. She made another stab at blanketing her thoughts before her imagination got the best of her.

She pulled a sweater from his closet and then decided to grab his heavy jacket in case the weather took an early winter turn.

She'd just left the bathroom when there was a sharp knock at the door.

"Mr. Murdock? Are you in there?" an unfamiliar woman's voice penetrated the thick wood.

Maggie hesitated for a moment, wondering if there was any chance of ignoring the knock. The doorknob jiggled and she heard the sound of keys rattling.

It had to be the landlady.

Maggie didn't have time to think. She pasted a polite smile on her face and opened the door to greet an older woman with purplish gray hair.

The woman jerked back. "Oh my gracious." She clasped her hand to her chest. "You frightened me."

"I'm sorry. I didn't mean to startle you. You must be Mrs. Harris."

"I know who I am. Who are you?"

"I'm Maggie Ben—" she caught her faux pas just in time. "Murdock." She hoped Mrs. Harris didn't notice her stuttering.

"You're the wife?"

It was all Maggie could do to nod her head. The words of deceit were locked in the back of her throat.

If anything, the landlady eyed her with even more suspicion. "I've never seen you over here before. Seems awfully strange for a man to marry someone who's never been to his own home. How do I know you're the missus?"

"Would you like to see some identification or perhaps you want to call Sergeant Wylie Jameson at the Pendleton Police Department. He'll verify my identity. You can use Griff's cell phone."

Mrs. Harris didn't take up the offer to use the

phone. Neither did she seem convinced. "Ever since the shooting, I've been locking the house whenever I come and go, never knowing if someone was going to show up here and start shooting at me."

"I'm sure you're in no danger."

"You're sure? You know who shot Mr. Murdock?"

"The police are diligently pursuing all leads. Whoever shot Mr. Murdock will be behind bars soon."

"Humpf." Mrs. Harris folded her arms. "If they're so smart, then how come Mr. Murdock got himself shot? Seems to me that no one is safe if a cop can't take care of himself."

Before Maggie could respond, the landlady lowered her arms and waved an accusatory finger in Maggie's direction. "Then I come home and hear you rummaging around. I thought someone had broken into Mr. Murdock's. He had told me to keep an eye on things until he got back. How do I know who's a crook or who's not?"

From the way the older woman rattled on, Maggie could see Mrs. Harris was definitely working herself into a state. Maggie resorted to the patient tone she'd used with Aunt Jessica. "Mrs. Harris, I don't believe you're in any danger."

"Why not? Mr. Murdock was shot, wasn't he? Since he's not dead, or..." Her voice trailed off and her eyes widened. "Oh no. Is he dead? Are you collecting his things?"

She tried to peer around Maggie's shoulder to see what she had been doing inside the room.

Maggie used her body as a shield to ward off the woman's prying eyes. "No, Mr. Murdock isn't dead."

Desperate to get rid of her unwanted visitor, she placed a reassuring hand on the woman's arm. "Griff just wanted me to pick up a few of his things."

"That looks like more than a few things." The older woman frowned at her suspiciously. "Mr. Murdock's not trying to skip out on his rent, is he? Is that why you're cleaning out his things?"

"No, he'll pay his rent at the regular time."

"When is he coming back?"

"He'll contact you."

"Why can't you tell me?"

"I don't know when he'll be released from hospital."

"What about his mail? Maybe I should take it to him, just to make sure he's doing all right."

"I'm sure he would appreciate your visit once the quarantine has been lifted."

"Quarantine?" Mrs. Harris took a step backward, as if Maggie was spewing germs. "He's sick? I thought he had been shot."

"There's been a viral breakout at the hospital, and they're limiting the number of visitors to the hospital."

"How come you haven't been quarantined?"

"I'm immune." The lies were literally tripping off her tongue. Before Mrs. Harris could form another question, Maggie said, "I'll have him contact you as soon as he's up and about. Would that be acceptable?"

"What about his mail? I don't want to be responsible for nondelivery."

"Forward it to the department. I'm sure Griff will want to reimburse you for your trouble."

Maggie started to close the door, hoping the woman would take the hint and leave.

Mrs. Harris wasn't about to be pushed out. She thrust her foot in the doorway. "You tell him I've got a waiting list for this room and it would be common courtesy for him to let me know if I need to get a new tenant."

Only after she got her final word in did she pivot and close the door behind her.

Maggie sagged against the wall in relief. She quickly relatched the door, a flimsy attempt to ward off any more sudden intrusions.

Within minutes, she'd finished packing, eager to put distance between herself and the nosy landlady.

Before she could unlatch the door, the phone rang.

Should she answer it?

There was no answering machine.

After the third ring, she grabbed the receiver. "Hello?"

The person on the other end didn't respond, even though Maggie heard breathing. "Is anyone there?"

"Are you Mrs. Murdock? Mrs. Griff Murdock?" an unfamiliar voice whispered.

"Yes, I am."

A long pause answered.

"Hello?" she asked. "Who's there?"

A distinct click reverberated on the other end.

Maggie slowly recradled the phone. There was something eerie about the voice.

Who would care whether or not she was married to Griff? An old girlfriend?

When they'd embarked on the engagement, Griff had claimed he hadn't seriously dated anyone in over a year.

Maggie attempted to shake off her increasing jitteriness as she gathered up the rest of Griff's things and headed toward the door.

She jumped as a phone rang. The sound came from the small pocket-sized phone Griff had insisted she take with her. The suitcase slipped out her hands as she fumbled for it.

"Maggie?"

She recognized Griff's deep voice and almost sagged with relief.

"Who else would it be?" Then Maggie realized how snappish she sounded. She never thought she'd be relieved to hear the sound of Griff Murdock's voice. "Sorry. I'm just a little frazzled."

"What happened?"

"I just had a run in with your landlady, and I intercepted a creepy phone call. Other than that, life is rosy."

"Who called?"

"Someone who didn't seem to be too happy about me being married to you. I figure it was an old girlfriend."

Griff didn't say anything right away. Then she heard him repeating what she said to someone else.

"Is that Wylie?" she asked.

"Yeah. He wants us to get out of town as soon as possible. Is Christine still with you?"

Maggie checked out the window. "She's parked across the street."

"How soon can you get here?"

"I'm almost finished, although I couldn't find your pajamas or robe."

"I usually don't need them."

"Oh."

"You can stop and pick up a bathrobe and pajamas at Mert's Store. I've got an account there."

"What size?"

"Large."

Maggie could hear his rich amusement. She refused to give him the satisfaction of knowing he was getting under her skin. Fortunately, she was alone where no one else could see the flush warming her cheeks. "Anything else?" she asked, keeping her tone as cool and impersonal as possible. She didn't want to think about how wifely this conversation sounded.

"Not for me."

She snapped shut the cell phone and gathered up Griff's belongings one more time.

Mrs. Harris seemed to be waiting for Maggie to appear as she stepped into the hall. "You tell Mr. Murdock that I'll be sleeping with a gun under my pillow."

"You got a license for it?"

Mrs. Harris sniffed. "My nephew gave me this gun for my own protection. Are you threatening to arrest me when real criminals are out on the streets terrorizing law-abiding citizens?"

"Law-abiding citizens carry registered guns."

The landlady humpfed and spun on her toe. She

entered a room at the end of the hall and slammed the door behind her.

Maggie didn't waste any time. She strode down the sidewalk and gestured to Christine. "Pop the trunk."

As soon as she threw the suitcase into the trunk, she hopped into the passenger seat. "Drive as fast as it's legal."

Christine didn't hesitate. "You okay?" she asked.

"I will be as soon as I'm out of range from Mrs. Harris."

"A gossip?"

"The worst kind. Wylie should hire her. She'd make a first-class interrogator."

Christine shuddered. "Not while I'm working there."

"You've met her?"

"Once."

"Once is all it takes."

"Yep."

"We've got to make another stop before we pick up my things."

Inside Mert's Store, Maggie found everything without assistance. She deliberately chose unappealing colors in both items even though she hoped to never see Griff in either of them. At the checkout she was blessed with a salesclerk who was more interested in peeling off her nail polish than inclined to question Maggie about her purchases or chatting. Maggie was in and out of the store in seven minutes flat.

Her last stop, at her apartment, didn't take much time, either. She'd already had a head start on her packing. She simply resorted her suitcase to take only those items that would be appropriate for northern Wisconsin. Besides jeans, shirts and toiletries, she decided to bring her sewing machine and the doll fabric she'd just purchased. The days would get long, and she'd need to keep busy.

Fortunately she didn't have to make arrangements for the rest of her belongings. Her landlord was scheduled to be gone for the next three months while he visited his children. He had told her there was no hurry for her to move out.

Locking the door behind her, she stowed her gear into her station wagon that was parked in the yard behind the house. Then she retrieved Griff's suitcase from the trunk of Christine's car.

Flashing a "let's go" wave toward Christine, she drove back toward the hospital with the police car keeping pace behind her. Through her rearview mirror, Maggie kept her own eye on any suspicious activity behind them. She stuck to residential streets, which were quieter and made it easier to spot a shadow.

It occurred to her that this might be the last time she'd have to herself for the next few weeks. Was it too late to find another solution instead of fleeing to northern Wisconsin?

An African safari? A trip to Siberia? A dogsled ride to the Arctic?

As tempting as each of these escapes sounded, she knew that unless the shooter came forward and turned himself in, she was stuck.

And that's just how she saw it, too.

Stuck going on a honeymoon with Griff.

Chapter 6

They slipped out of town just after midnight, with not even the hospital staff alerted to their exit.

Wylie planned to smooth over any explanations after Maggie and Griff were safely out of range.

Maggie navigated the highway, too conscious of Griff's unrelenting presence in the back of the car. His cast made sitting in the passenger seat an impossibility. She couldn't decide if that was to her advantage or not.

"Dim your lights." Griff's voice growled a warning.

Maggie's mouth tightened as she flicked the hand control.

Damn! He was already getting in the way of her normal good sense. As soon as the beam responded to a lower wattage, she said, "Why don't I drive and you sleep? It's a good four hours to Jonas Falls."

"I don't sleep in cars."

"Fine. I'll sleep and you drive. Let me know when we get there."

"I would if I could."

"Right. You can't and I can."

"Touchy, aren't you?"

"Only toward grouches and back seat drivers."

For a moment he didn't respond. As the tires of the vehicle hummed against the pavement, she could feel his watchfulness even though she couldn't see him.

"I guess I deserved that," he finally said. "I'm not used to relinquishing control."

"And you don't trust me," she said flatly.

"Any reason why I should?"

"I've given you no reason not to," she countered.

A voice in her head urged her to ignore Griff. Normally she'd feel sorry for someone with two bullet wounds in him and would overlook any crankiness.

But Griff had always brought out the worst in her. Despite the roominess of the station wagon, Griff seemed to fill every corner. There were no buffers like the ones they'd had during their so-called engagement. The other officers were safely out of range. It was just she and her nemesis. And the tension in the back of her neck was killing her.

"Relax. I'm not going to grab the wheel," Griff drawled.

Her laugh contained no humor. "You expect me to trust you when you can't trust me?"

"With my leg in a cast and my arm out of commission, it wouldn't be smart for me to try anything that would put us both in danger. I'm not looking for a return visit to the hospital. How about calling a truce?''

''Do you think that's possible?''

''It's either that or one of us will kill the other one.''

He said it so matter-of-factly that she couldn't contain the smile that turned up the corners of her mouth.

''That's a possibility I hadn't considered.'' She flexed her fingers, attempting to loosen the death grip she had on the steering wheel. ''If one of us took out the other, then we wouldn't have to hole up in the north woods of Wisconsin.''

''I should warn you,'' Griff said. ''I've gotten pretty good with this crutch.''

She shook her head. ''Could have fooled me. You didn't look too steady with it when we left the hospital.''

''Don't tempt me, Bennington.''

''Say the word, Murdock, and I'll stop the car. We can get this over with right now.''

He suddenly started to laugh. ''Why do I have a feeling you'd do it, too?''

''Because I'm BJ's daughter.''

''And you hate my guts.''

''Forever and ever.''

The insane conversation bordered on the macabre. She found herself feeling amazingly relaxed. As relaxed as she could be with Griff sitting behind her.

He sighed. ''I suppose Wylie wouldn't take kindly to having to deal with another murder and murder victim.''

''It could delay the investigation.''

''Can't have that.''

''Ditto.''

For the next few miles, silence reigned. They passed through two small towns, and she was careful to maintain the speed limit. They didn't want to alert anyone to their presence.

As soon as they entered the open highway again, Maggie resumed her speed. She heard Griff shift in the seat behind her. ''Do you want me to pull over?''

''No, I'm just trying to find a comfortable position.''

She felt him bump the back of her seat and muffle a curse.

''What the heck is this thing at my feet?''

''A sewing machine.''

''Why did you bring that?''

''I'm not going to sit around and twiddle my thumbs for the next month and a half.''

''You're going to sew a new wardrobe?''

''No. I'm making doll clothes.''

''Doll clothes? You play with dolls?''

''You'd rather I played with guns?'' she asked.

She heard him shift in the seat behind her. ''Sorry. I asked for that one, didn't I? Guess I'm having trouble getting the hang of being married again.''

With the aid of the dashboard lights, Maggie's gaze met his through the rearview mirror. ''I'd forgotten you were married before. Is there something I should know?''

Stilted silence met her query. The light atmosphere of a few minutes earlier disappeared.

She couldn't help but ponder why he never talked

about his marriage. Maggie vaguely recalled he'd been married when he moved to Pendleton. His wife had been dark-haired and had worn a chronic petulant expression the few times Maggie had seen her. Within the year Griff's wife died, the result of a car accident. Maggie had heard rumors that Griff's wife had run away with another man. But her father would never talk about it.

Maggie wasn't surprised that the marriage had been on the verge of dissolution. Griff was married to his job, just as Maggie's father had been. There were few good marriages on the police force. The brotherhood always prevailed over other relationships.

Had that been what had happened to Griff's marriage? Had his wife resented competing with the department for his attention?

Curiosity sparked question upon question, even as she kept alert to any possible tails.

The road behind them stayed quiet, however, while her head continued to work overtime.

She knew that Griff dated occasionally. There was no doubt about his sexual orientation. However, he never brought the same woman to any of the police social functions.

Did Griff still love his wife? Did he feel a sense of betrayal? Or loss? Was that why he'd never married again?

Careful, Maggie, you can't afford to take an interest in the man. She refused to let a man like Griff get under her skin. If she was going to survive the next couple of weeks, she needed to bolster her barriers.

The armored quiet presiding over the car seemed

like an ominous foreplay to what lie ahead when she faced cohabiting with the man she'd resented her entire adult life.

The cabin, nestled at the end of a deserted stretch of road, remained invisible until they turned the last bend and their headlights illuminated a shadowy building.

By the time Maggie pulled the vehicle into the solitary garage, Griff was clenching his teeth, bracing for the agony of moving his numb limb. He didn't think he'd been more uncomfortable in his life. Yet he wasn't looking forward to having Maggie assist him out of the car.

According to Wylie, the caretakers took a holiday as soon as the summer tourists fled back to their winter homes, so Wylie hadn't had to make explanations to anyone other than the local sheriff about their sudden appearance.

Maggie turned off the ignition and opened the car door to assist him.

"Get the bags out of the back," he said tersely. "I can manage myself."

"My hero." Her voice was every bit as sarcastic as his. "You think you can get up those steps without help, Big Guy, go ahead."

She didn't try to talk him out of his obstinacy. Turning her back on him, she yanked open the gate and pulled several bags out of the back end.

As soon as she climbed the steps and unlocked the cabin, Griff tried to wedge his body out of the cramped seat. His limbs and joints were stiffer than he'd thought.

Maggie reappeared as he hefted his body from the back seat. Unfortunately, his crutch was out of his reach.

Without saying a word, Maggie handed it to him and then returned to grab another load of stuff.

Griff faced the flight of steps and buried a groan. They were every bit as intimidating as if he were about to tackle the climb to the top of the Sears Tower. He took one step and nearly pitched face-first into the uneven ground. His normal leg was still protesting from the muscle cramps of being cooped up.

Struggling to maintain his balance, he suddenly found his arm lifted and a small pair of shoulders braced against his ribs.

Maggie's face lifted toward his. The brilliant green militancy of her gaze dared him to challenge her assistance.

"Ready?" she asked.

With the steely lock he had on his jaw, he could do little more than nod. The steep awkward steps weren't nearly as jarring as the heat and firm curves of Maggie's body pressed against him. Her thin shirt didn't provide any kind of buffer. She'd taken off her jacket before they'd started out. He'd known the next few weeks would test his sanity. He just hadn't wanted to realize how much.

"The architect of this staircase had a twisted sense of humor," Maggie said.

"Either that or he liked small people," Griff

agreed, relieved at Maggie's attempt to keep things light and impersonal.

Without her help, it would have taken him a hell of a lot longer to ascend the narrow width of the stairs.

He was surprised how strong and steady Maggie felt beneath his arm as they conquered the first step.

"Remind me that I get to put a bullet in the shooter's leg when Wylie nabs the coward," he said breathing heavily.

"I think that's too merciful." She didn't flinch as he leaned even more heavily.

By the time they reached the top, they were both panting and it had nothing to do with the caged heat of the early autumn night.

Griff readjusted his crutch. "I think I can make it from here."

"All right." Maggie wedged the door and stood aside. "The lights are on. You can take the bedroom."

The cold absence after Maggie removed her warm support jarred Griff. This sharp sense of loss he could do without. It was a heck of a beginning.

Griff lowered himself onto a kitchen chair as Maggie made her final trip outside. He heard the sound of the locks being engaged in her car, followed by the garage doors swinging shut.

Then she came into the cabin. As soon as the door closed behind her the atmosphere inside the small cabin became closer.

She set Griff's suitcase on the floor and perched a bag of groceries on the short kitchen counter. She scanned the room critically. "I'll close those window blinds so the lights can't be seen from the road."

Griff hated feeling useless as she leaned across and yanked the cord. The worst part was his inability to look away as her short-sleeved sweater hitched up to expose the smooth creamy skin of her lower back.

"That should do it, don't you think?"

Her question caught him unaware. For a second he couldn't think what she was talking about. When her gaze narrowed suspiciously, he made a quick recovery. "What about the window at the back?"

"There's no window covering. I'll check the closets for an extra blanket, but it might not be necessary since that side faces the woods."

"This place is already stuffy," Griff noted.

Shutting out any more light would make the room uncomfortably close.

The cabin had been designed to maximize efficiency. The cedar-lined walls housed a tight kitchen alcove, a one-step-you're-in or one-step-you're-out bathroom and a small bedroom in addition to the main room that wasn't much bigger than a den.

The last thing they needed was for their living quarters to become cozier than it already was.

He noticed Maggie was trying to keep her eyes averted from him. Awkwardness riddled the silence.

He didn't like how he was suddenly so aware of her.

Maggie lifted the grocery bags from the table and moved them to the small counter. "I'll put these away if you want to get ready for bed."

"You take the bedroom."

"What about—"

He cut her off. "I don't want to keep you awake."

Her eyes found his. Whatever she saw there must have convinced her it was best not to argue. She pointed to his suitcase. "Do you need help with some of this?"

"Leave it for now. I'll find a place for it later."

"Fine. I'll pull out the sofa bed."

He nodded and made an effort to look away as she flipped the cushions off the couch and pulled on the strap to unfold the mattress. Under its own volition, Griff's gaze slipped back to see her sweater move upward again. His mouth dried and he clutched the handle of his crutch, purposefully emptying his mind as she finished smoothing the blankets.

After she found a pillow in the closet and tossed it on the sofa, she tugged her sweater back into place before picking up her own bag. "I guess if that's all—"

"It is."

"Do you need help with anything?"

"No."

Her gaze flickered from the bed to him. "What about your clothes?"

Griff's mouth twisted into something that should have been a smile, but clearly wasn't. "Anxious to start performing your wifely duties?"

She lifted her chin and gave him a frigid glare. "That's not what I meant."

"I don't need you to tuck me in, Bennington."

Griff's patience sounded decidedly strained.

"Who said I was volunteering, Murdock?" A trace of red eased up her neckline. She didn't look at him as she crossed the room. "I'll see you in the morning."

Griff found himself alone, left to deal with his own bad temper. Using their last names reminded them both to be professional. But the earthy surroundings seemed designed to undermine his intent.

He was going to have to find a way to keep his mind on his job.

Using his good hand, he unsnapped his jeans. Removing them, however, wasn't an option. Even if he could struggle out of them and into the pajamas Maggie bought, he wouldn't be able to sleep. And he figured it was safer for everyone if he didn't shuck his jeans. His limbs might be a little worse for the wear, but there wasn't a thing wrong with his libido.

He was much too conscious of Maggie moving around in the other room.

Finally, all was quiet.

Too quiet.

Despite the wee early morning hour, Griff suspected Maggie wasn't asleep anymore than he was.

Hell, he wanted to smash down the door and that made him even more frustrated.

She was his so-called wife. In name only. Yet from the moment he'd gotten into the vehicle with her, he'd had a hard time remembering that fact.

He'd noticed how the dashboard lights caught the red in her hair. Whenever they'd pass under the street lights, he'd catch sight of the creamy arch of her neck and wondered how it would feel beneath his touch.

Forget it, Griff. She was exactly the kind of woman

he had vowed to stay away from. Hadn't he learned his lesson when Sonja died?

He'd thought he had.

Now he wasn't so sure.

How many times would he have to remind himself over the next month and a half that Maggie Bennington was off-limits?

Eternity was starting to seem shorter than the weeks ahead.

Chapter 7

Throughout the remainder of the night, Maggie counted every hour. By the time dawn crept through the thicket of trees guarding the cabin, she was exhausted. It was only then she allowed the tension to roll from her exhausted body, and she slid into a dreamless sleep.

Several hours later she awoke.

She lay listening for any sounds coming from the other room.

There were none.

Had Griff been able to sleep on that sofa bed? She didn't think comfort had ever been the primary purpose behind the design of sofa beds. But Griff had been insistent that he sleep on this one.

Had he worn the new pajamas she'd purchased?

Dare she venture out into the other room in case he hadn't?

The last thing she needed to do was see more of Griff Murdock than she had to.

Basic needs finally forced her to get out of bed. By the time she cautiously inched out of the bedroom, she had showered and dressed.

Slowly she eased open the door and came to an abrupt stop. Little had changed since the night before. Griff was propped in the big leather chair next to the neatly made sofa bed.

Griff didn't look as if he'd weathered the night well. He still wore the same clothes he'd worn the day before. His eyes sported deep sunken hollows, darker than twin cesspools. His jaw looked gritty with a shadowy telltale sign of whiskers.

Had he slept at all?

His shuttered expression successfully discouraged her from asking.

She searched for something to break the ice. "What would you like for breakfast?"

"It's past noon."

"So it is. What would you like for lunch?"

"Is cooking in your job description?"

"No. Is it in yours?"

Griff grappled with his crutch and hauled himself to his feet. "I'll take care of myself."

She gritted her teeth. He was determined to be obstinate. "Whatever."

"When is Wylie coming?"

"He said he'd try to get away today. If he can't, he'll be here tomorrow."

The shadows on Griff's face turned grimmer.

As the silence lengthened, she sighed. "Was there something you needed?"

"I'd like to get out of these clothes."

Maggie peered at him through her eyelashes. Did he feel as uncomfortable as he looked?

Guilt cascaded over her as she recalled the ease of her own shower and the fact that she could move around on her own two feet. If she were in Griff's place, she'd probably be every bit as surly as he was. Maybe even more so.

She weighed her options and the possible repercussions. "The way I see it, you can stand there and growl at me the rest the day, making this situation more untenable than it already is. Or you can allow me to help you." She paused to give him a chance to consider the wisdom of her suggestions, before adding, "It's your call. How desperate are you to have a shave and wear clean clothes? Enough to lower your manly pride and let me help?"

Griff's gray eyes continued to be remote. He seemed to be trying to drill holes through her, perhaps to determine if she had any ulterior motives. She met his gaze, withstanding his silent assault. "What's it going to be, Murdock?"

Finally he said, "These clothes are starting to get ripe."

"Is that a yes?"

He nodded.

She pushed aside the peanut butter jar she'd pulled from the cupboard and braced herself. If she was going to help him, she intended to be as businesslike as possible. "Fine. I'll help you get out of your shirt. Before we shave would you like to—"

"I'll take it from there."

"Right."

The tension writhed between them, tangible and menacing. Griff's clenched jaw made Maggie long to run in the other direction.

Neither of them moved.

The clock struck one o'clock.

Shoving aside her misgivings, she walked toward Griff. "Are you ready to escape that shirt? I'd like to get some work done while it's still daylight."

He grunted.

She began with the buttons, trying to ignore the heat of Griff's body. She could feel his gaze on her face and struggled to keep her fingers steady.

She searched for a neutral subject. "Why are you anxious for Wylie to arrive?"

"He's supposed to be bringing files of old cases."

"What cases?"

"Just ours and BJ's."

Her fingers stilled for a moment. "Why Dad's?"

"We need to cover every possible lead. It's a long shot that the shooting had anything to do with your dad, but it's a connection we can't overlook since BJ was the common bond between both of us before the wedding. Besides, it'll give us something to do."

"Sounds like a good idea." Her voice sounded husky and unnatural to her own ears as she helped tug the shirt off his powerful shoulders and revealed the firm muscles.

Aargh! He was too beautiful to be real. Hardly daring to breathe, her fingers shook as her skin bounced off his radiating heat. She unhooked the last button and released a long breath.

For once Griff seemed fresh out of cutting comments, and she was profoundly grateful. She carefully pulled the shirt off his injured arm and noticed his breathing was even more jagged than her own. "Am I hurting you?"

"Not in the way you mean."

Her gaze tangled with his. His eyes reminded her of Arctic glaciers. They were smoky and intense, making her much too conscious that she was a woman alone with a very attractive man.

The shirt slipped from her fingers. She leaned down and snatched it up. "Where would you like me to put this?"

"Toss it by the empty suitcase. I assume we'll have to do laundry eventually."

"Yes." She kept her head turned away from him. It was safer.

He didn't move away. Turning, her shirt caught on the edge of the table and exposed her midriff before she could tug it free.

Griff's good hand grabbed her arm. Without asking her permission, he lifted the edge of her shirt to reveal the purplish marks she'd striven to hide.

"What the heck are these?" he asked. "Where did you get these bruises?"

She dislodged his hand by stepping out of his reach. "It's the price of the job. You weren't the only one who came away with war wounds from the wedding."

"You never said anything."

''Why should I? Getting a cut or scrape on duty isn't a big deal.'' At his scowl, she sighed. ''They're fading now.''

''Why didn't you mention this?''

''I did. I told you to get off me. Remember?''

''You're being flip.''

''And you're overreacting.''

Griff's lips pressed into a fine line. Finally he raked his hand through his hair. ''Sorry. I guess I'm having trouble getting used to this whole situation.''

She chose not to mention her own misgivings. They'd been here less than a day and already the tension was becoming unbearable. ''Did you need something else?''

''Could you hand me that crutch?''

She did what he asked and then slipped past him to the kitchen. ''I'll make those sandwiches.''

The door closed behind him. She flinched when she heard the sound of the crutch falling. The bathroom was tiny by any standards. With the size of Griff's cast, he was doubly handicapped. But she wasn't willing to bait his temper by offering to assist him.

She heard a muffled curse, followed by the sound of water running. Only then did her muscles relax some of her tension.

She hoped Wylie would get here sooner than later. They were going to desperately need someone to diffuse the electrical undercurrents between them. The danger was either they'd lunge for each other or kill each other.

She wasn't placing any bets on which one would happen first.

* * *

Griff sponged himself off as best he could with his left hand. The scruff on his face was another story. He wasn't fond of the caveman look, but there was no way he could control a razor without slicing his jaw open. The only other alternative was to ask Maggie's assistance. He hated being beholden to anyone.

Especially Maggie.

He turned off the water and stared hard into the mirror.

Maggie Bennington had always been a thorn in his side. Putting a razor in her hand seemed a foolhardy risk. Yet he wasn't nearly as worried about a razor in her hand as he was about his reaction to her touch. He'd been in a state of arousal every time she got close. How much more pressure could he take?

Gazing at his grizzled mug in the bathroom mirror, he considered his options.

Could he stand looking like Paul Bunyan for the next six weeks?

His face itched at the thought.

Hell!

Balancing himself, he yanked open the door. "Maggie?"

She came cautiously around the corner and lifted an eyebrow at his query.

"How steady is your hand?" he asked.

Her eyes flitted from his face to the shaver sitting next to the sink. She didn't look anymore comfortable with the notion than he did with asking.

She tilted her head. "Some women are partial to furry men."

"I doubt it. Can you help me out?"

She set down the knife she'd been using to butter the bread. "There's not enough room in there for both of us. Let's do it in the kitchen."

"There's not much room in there, either."

"No. But at least there's the table."

"Right."

He hobbled across the floor and eased into one of the cushioned wood chairs, easing his arm onto the table.

Maggie set the razor and shaving cream next to him and critically scanned his face. "You'd have a heavy beard if you'd let this grow. You could probably enter and win an old-timers' contest."

"Looking for an excuse to get out of this?"

His needling caused her to lift her chin. "Watch it, Murdock. I'm savoring the anticipation of putting a sharp blade against your throat, and I refuse to be rushed."

"Don't get any ideas. I can still take you down, cast or not."

She didn't respond to his baiting as she picked up the shaving cream and sprayed foam into her hand, then coated his face. "Lift your head."

Prudence won over the urge to badger her further. Griff kept his eyes trained on her face as she raised the razor and took a gentle swipe across his jaw.

A reluctant admiration burned in his gut at her concentration and willingness to agree to this whole scenario.

Throughout the weeks of the engagement, she'd enacted her role as the happy fiancé without complaint.

But everything she'd been required to do had been in social situations that had allowed her to keep a respectable distance. Anyone else might not have recognized the polite façade that she'd hidden behind had masked a disdain for her proposed groom. They hadn't needed to like each other, just act as though they did. Only he had been aware of the way she'd stiffen whenever he brushed against her or reached for her hand. It had amused him at the time. He'd enjoyed seeing the flash of irritation when he played the affectionate suitor.

Now she had the upper hand.

The enforced intimacy of the tiny cabin was a dangerous breeding ground, much more threatening than acting a role in front of all their peers at the bridal showers, bachelor parties and social events leading up to the wedding. Inside the microscopic quarters, there wasn't anyone else to defuse the combustion between them.

Griff watched Maggie place her cool fingers against his neck to tilt his head and sensed the tight lock she had on her emotions. She could feel the danger as much as he could.

They probably would have been safer taking on the shooter face-to-face.

How long would Maggie stick this out?

She'd all but declared him her personal enemy years ago. She'd resented his relationship with her father. And that had led to a silent war between them, even though Griff had never had any urge to fight her.

BJ had been his partner. They'd worked together well.

But for all BJ's strengths as a good cop, he'd never understood what it took to be a good father.

Griff couldn't deny that Maggie had all but been abandoned. When she hadn't been able to get her father's attention in a positive way, such as good grades, becoming a class officer or succeeding in school sports, she'd tried to get it by acting out. First there had been arguments. Then she started staying out late and sneaking off to forbidden parties. She hung out with kids who were on the fast track to becoming career criminals. BJ raged and threatened. But he didn't give Maggie what she hungered for—his time.

Griff had tried to stay clear of the family situation until Maggie was caught shoplifting.

BJ had been out of the office when the call came in. Fortunately Griff knew the owner of the store. He worked a deal in which Maggie would volunteer her free time to pick up trash from the parking lot for two months. When they left the store, Maggie had balked about getting into Griff's car until he threatened to handcuff her and lock her up. She'd gotten into the car. Then he took her home.

Once they got there, he'd followed her into the house.

"We need to talk."

"I have nothing to say to you." She'd been defiant.

There was less than ten years between their ages, yet Griff had felt old enough to be her grandfather.

"Tough. I'm still carrying the handcuffs."

She'd kept her seat but didn't bother to mask her hate for him. "Say what you have to say, then get out of here."

He stood up and walked to the refrigerator. "Want something to drink?"

"I'll take a beer."

He brought her a root beer instead. When she refused to take it, he said, "You're going about this all wrong, you know."

Her gaze narrowed. "What are you talking about?"

"You want your dad's attention." He set the glass on the table next to her. "Hanging out with those losers who are stealing from hard-working business owners isn't going to bring your dad home at night."

She lifted her chin. "You're just saying that because you want Dad to spend all his time with you."

"That's one possibility. Or maybe I'm just looking out for my own neck."

"This has nothing to do with you."

"Wanna bet?"

"He's my father," she raged at him.

"He's my partner."

"Big deal."

"It is a big deal if my partner is worried sick about his kid and doesn't have his full attention on a punk brandishing a gun. Not only is that dangerous to me, it's dangerous to your dad." He paused only briefly. "Is that what you want, Maggie?"

She straightened in the chair. The rebellious thrust of her chin quivered as his words hit home.

Whatever his personal opinion of Maggie was, Griff had been right about her overwhelming love for her father. She never wanted her actions to put BJ in harm's way. From that day on, she'd made a hundred and eighty degree turn.

BJ had been pleased that Maggie suddenly became the model student again. Later, he'd been busting his buttons when his only child chose to go to the police academy and then join the department.

But BJ never knew how to show that pride and love to Maggie. There were too many distractions and demands on her father's time for Maggie to get what she needed or desired.

Was that why Maggie ultimately left the department? Had she taken her revenge against her father?

Even then Griff had tried to keep an emotional distance, until he'd seen his friend and partner fall apart after Maggie moved away. Griff didn't hide his blame. When Maggie joined the police department she'd made a promise. Her reneging had killed her father.

That's what Griff had believed.

Had he been wrong all those years ago to steer Maggie toward the department, building his partner's hopes? BJ had been left with nothing when Maggie walked.

Now as he watched her concentration and the careful way she handled the razor, taking care not to nick him, he wondered if there were more to the story than he knew.

BJ had never tried to dissuade Maggie from leaving, which was very unusual for his blustering partner, who'd never made a secret of his opinions about his daughter's choices, her slipups or her friends. Yet Griff clearly recalled the day he'd learned that Maggie was leaving.

She'd been absent from the department for almost

a week. He'd assumed she was on vacation. BJ had been short-tempered while she'd been gone.

Griff and BJ were driving to Chicago to testify in an abduction and murder case when the older man tersely announced that Maggie wouldn't be returning. She had decided to transfer to a small-town department. It wasn't unusual for an officer to move into a different jurisdiction, but it was for a lower-ranking position with less money. And she was leaving her father. Had she given up her desire to get closer to her only parent?

Griff, being true to his own convictions, hadn't pressed for answers to the questions burning in his head.

Now Griff wondered about the pieces of the puzzle that were missing. Neither Maggie or BJ had acted in character.

Maggie stepped back and eyed her work critically. Being this close, he could see the softness of her lips that contrasted with the brilliant green in her eyes. If he were any other man, he'd want to make those eyes go dewy with fiery passion.

"Do you know that you have one ear longer than the other?" she asked.

Griff blinked, as her question pulled him from his lustful thoughts. He cleared his throat. "It's part of my sex appeal."

"Pretty sure of yourself, aren't you?"

He ran a hand over the now-smooth edge of his jaw. "Let's just say I'm not too worried about it one way or the other."

"Really?" She started cleaning off the table.

"You're not worried about what women think of you?"

He didn't answer for a long moment. Then he awkwardly found his footing and angled his crutch under his arm. "There's always someone who doesn't like something about you. If it's not your looks, it's the clothes you wear, the company you keep, the car you drive or the partner you have."

At the hint of her father, a curtain descended over Maggie's face, wiping clear any hint of her emotions. She presented her back to him. "I think I'll check the shed to see if there's a couple of fishing poles."

"I'm not much of a threat to the fish."

"Then I'll look for one pole."

Griff knew he should let her go. But the questions he'd brushed aside a year ago wouldn't let him. "We're going to have to talk about your dad sometime."

A familiar stubbornness took residence on her face. "I have a better idea, why don't we talk about your personal life instead. What went wrong with your marriage?"

"We ended it. There's nothing to talk about it."

"Ditto."

Without waiting for his response, she jerked open the door and fled the cabin.

He heard her descend the steps. If she thought this was the end, she was sorely mistaken.

He wanted to know every secret that Maggie was hiding. His investigative instincts were the only talent he had that could quench the desire churning within him.

What she didn't realize was that his probing questions were safer than the other investigation he was hungering to spearhead.

Despite his growing questions about why Maggie had left her father and the department, Griff couldn't quit thinking about Maggie's sweet curves, and her soft, soft skin.

Baiting her had become a matter of survival and sanity.

He feared he'd developed a fatal fascination with one Maggie Bennington.

Chapter 8

Maggie didn't realize she was running until she reached the dock. She stopped at the water's edge and tried to catch her breath.

Her hands came up to her face and she felt the blushing warmth. Lord, what had she been thinking in agreeing to hide out in the small cabin with Griff?

Danger had been a part of her life for as long as she remembered.

But handling a gun or facing an inner city gang were not nearly as perilous as living in the close proximity of Griff Murdock.

It didn't matter if he had a pair of ears that didn't match, or was handicapped by a broken leg and an injured shoulder. He oozed sex appeal.

Maggie had had few relationships over the course of the years. Every relationship had been patterned after the one she'd had with her only parent. The men she'd dated had been every bit as self-absorbed as her father had been. She fell for men who were inaccessible to her emotionally. When she finally admitted she was a breathing cliché, she quit. She dated here and there. But she didn't look for attachments. She was finally on the brink of living life on her own terms.

If for that reason and none other, she'd never get involved with Griff Murdock, she reminded herself.

She wasn't ashamed to use the memory of her father as a wedge between her and Griff. Her father owed her that shield.

Now, if she could only superimpose that logic over her senses. Her fingers still tingled from the touch of Griff's skin.

Damn him! An injured man shouldn't be so sexy, so male.

She tried to force his image from her mind and concentrate on the scene in front of her.

This part of Wisconsin radiated beauty no matter what time of year.

The overripe colors of summer were starting to give way to the vibrant hues of autumn. There would be another healthy surge of tourists during the weekends ahead to view the leaf change. And when the trees were bare and the snow fell, there would be people pursuing the winter sports: blazing new trails with their cross-country skis or revving up their snowmobiles.

Normally, she'd count her blessings that she was here between seasons after the summer residents had hightailed it back to Chicago, leaving peace and privacy in their wake.

But the peace and privacy were exactly what she didn't need right now.

Her thoughts circled back to the man she'd left in the cabin.

Griff was considered a catch by some. Those broad shoulders made women think of strength and faithfulness. But she, of all people, knew appearances could be very deceiving.

The first time she'd ever met him, he'd been a rookie. Her father hadn't been eager for such a young partner. But within a week of the pairing, whatever reservations BJ had disappeared.

Maggie found herself alone again and again, competing with her father's jobs and ultimately with Griff for attention. Not even when she'd finally joined the Pendleton Police Department had their relationship changed.

"We should stick together."

The sound of Griff's voice made Maggie jump. She spun around to find Griff ten yards away from her. "How did you get down here?" she asked, flinching at the stupidity of her question. "You shouldn't be walking on that leg."

"The exercise will help it heal faster. Did you find the fishing pole?"

She shook her head. "I hadn't gotten that far."

Griff gazed over her shoulder at the small lake. A narrow wooden dock jutted twenty feet across the water. "I never realized Wylie had this place."

"His parents left him a little nest egg when they

died, so he bought the cabin. It was his true escape from the job. Very few people know about this place or his connection to it.''

''It's amazing he ever leaves.''

''He keeps talking about retiring, but I don't think he can turn his back on the job entirely.''

''Maybe you should consider opening your shop around here.''

She could feel the wistful smile tug at her mouth. ''I'd love to, but the retail trade fades out during the winter. Most of the shops are only open during the summer season. They close in the late fall.''

''It's a tough way to do business.''

''Yeah.''

For a brief moment they stood together looking at the scenic landscape. But for Maggie the tranquility had slipped away with Griff's sudden appearance.

She pointed to the makeshift shed that sat near the edge of the tree line. ''Wylie stores his fishing equipment in there.''

Without waiting for his response, she hiked the short distance to the small building. She fished the key from her pocket and unlocked the door.

Griff was sitting on the edge of the dock when she returned with a pole and tackle box.

He watched her expertly bait the hook and cast the fishing line into the water. He absently adjusted his arm in the sling and kept an eye on Maggie. She fished from the side of the dock that overlooked a patch of weeds.

''What kind of fish are you hoping to snare?''

''Smallmouth bass, mostly.''

"You don't need live bait?"

"I've had a lot of success with this hardheaded, soft-bodied lure. The natural swimming motion usually attracts a large variety of species."

"What other types live in these waters?"

"Largemouth bass, stripers, trout and a few others." Maggie reeled in her line and cast it again. The sun had risen high above the trees and caught the reddish glints in her hair.

He was amazed at how relaxed she had become. The tension that had riddled her expression had given way as she easily handled the rod in her hand. He didn't think he'd ever seen her this at ease or sure of herself. But then, she'd never let him get this close before.

"Maybe you should become a fishing guide."

She chuckled. Her expression curried an edge of mischief. "You trying to find me another job?"

He felt his own mouth turn up at the corners. "Just trying to connect all the dots."

"Ever the cop."

"Not everyone has all your hidden talents, Bennington. BJ never mentioned anything about fishing. Could he manage a rod and reel as well as you do?"

She shook her head. "Dad didn't like coming up here. He wasn't much for the great outdoors unless it involved chasing down a criminal. He hated bugs, birds and anything to do with wildlife."

"So you came up here with Wylie?"

"He was my godfather. Sometimes he seemed more like a parent than Dad did."

"Did you ever know your mother?"

Maggie shook her head. "She died of a brain aneurysm before I was a year old. Dad never would talk about her, so I know very little about who she was or what she liked to do."

"It was probably too painful for him to remember."

Her expression twisted. "That was Dad all right. If it was personal or emotional, he shut it down."

Any mention of BJ brought a distinct coolness to Maggie's expression. Griff strove to steer the conversation back to a neutral track. "What do you do after you catch something?"

"I throw them back in."

Griff rubbed his shoulder again.

"Is your arm bothering you?" Maggie asked.

"What?"

"You keep massaging it. Are you having some pain?"

He hadn't realized he'd been worrying his arm. "No. I don't like being restricted. I think I'd rather wear handcuffs."

"You want to borrow mine?"

Her playful comment tweaked him in a way he didn't expect. Her sassiness contained a sexy edge. Did she sense it, or was he the only one feeling the heat shimmering between them?

This was another side of Maggie he'd seldom seen. Around him, she wore a protective armor that hid her expressions. "Feeling pretty cocky, Bennington?" he asked. "Don't let this cast deceive you. I can still take you down."

"I don't think—" Her easiness disappeared. "Oh, shoot!"

"What's the matter?"

"My line is snagged on that branch."

Maggie set down her pole between two rocks so it wouldn't slip into the lake.

"What are you going to do?"

"Unsnag it."

Griff eyed the murky water. He wasn't much of a swimmer, even without the cast. If something should happen to her.... "Can't you just break it?"

"The water isn't that deep."

Without a backward glance, she carefully waded out into the water where the line stretched taut. She didn't seem bothered by her wet pants or shoes.

Griff recalled a time when his wife had gotten caught in a rainstorm. Getting her hair wet had been tantamount to braving an earthquake. Yet here was Maggie, unconcerned with her hair, feet or legs, venturing into a lake to save a fishing line.

Griff struggled to his feet and snugged the crutch to his side. Lord knows what he'd do if she dropped out of sight. He wanted to be alert, just in case.

Before he could hobble a foot, Maggie called, "Got it."

Griff stopped at the water's edge as Maggie emerged with her freed line.

She looked down at her wet legs and grimaced. "Guess I'd better change. Do you need help getting back?"

"I can manage."

Griff couldn't help but notice how the wet clothing clung to her body and revealed her shapely figure.

Lust packed a powerful punch and had him fighting to draw air into his lungs.

Fortunately Maggie was already agilely picking her way back to the cabin. He took his time following her.

She was quick and light on her feet, while he felt like he was carrying a ball and chain. Some rescuer he would have been.

Fortunately Maggie hadn't needed him.

He wondered why that bothered him.

By the middle of the afternoon, Griff's inactivity chafed and made him even more irritable.

After he'd arrived back inside the cabin, Maggie emerged from the shower. Wading into the lake hadn't slowed her down, he noted as she hauled her sewing machine to the table.

Before she pulled her fabric and patterns from one of the boxes she'd carried into the room, she set up the ironing board.

He checked his cell phone for messages but discovered that the digital service didn't reach the area.

"Wylie is going to have trouble contacting us."

At his comment, Maggie lifted her head from the scrap of cloth she was working on. "He can call the sheriff. We're not entirely out of touch."

"I wish he'd get here with those files."

Maggie didn't say anything as she lowered her head again.

"What are you doing?" Griff asked.

"I'm making pantaloons for two of the dolls I plan to display in my shop window."

"Do you ever sew real clothes?"

"Sometimes."

There was another lengthy pause. Then Griff said, "You'll make someone a great wife, Bennington."

"Are you trying to provoke me, Murdock?" She kept her tone even.

"Why is that a provocation? Don't you want to get married?"

"No."

"Why not?"

"Because I learned a long time ago that a woman can't count on a man."

The sound Griff made dripped with disbelief. "And a man can rely on a woman?"

Pressure started to build around Maggie's temples. "I suppose it depends on the woman."

"And the man."

She sighed and set down her sewing. "You have nothing to do so you want to start an argument?"

"It's not an argument. I'm curious to know why you haven't gotten married."

"Time, motive and opportunity. Take your pick."

"What about kids? Don't you like kids?"

The pressure crescendoed into a persistent drumbeat. "I adore children."

"You just don't want to have any of your own."

"I never said that."

"Then why don't you?"

"What?"

"Have children."

Maggie considered the man sitting across the room from her. His irritability wasn't surprising. The temperature inside the cabin had been climbing all afternoon. There was no air-conditioning and no wind to force a breeze through the open windows. Of all years to have a late September heat wave, why did it have to be this one?

Griff had changed his T-shirt but was still wearing the jeans with one pant leg slashed midway up his thigh to accommodate his cast. He'd run his fingers through his hair so many times that one side stood on end.

The rumpled look would be appealing if he didn't appear ready to push his fist down her throat.

They'd already covered topics that included the weather, politics, gender biases and the police department's budget cuts.

Now they had reverted back to personal subjects. She should be grateful he hadn't brought up her father's name.

"I don't intend to have children because I don't intend to get married."

"A lot of women are choosing to be single parents."

"Good for them. I, on the other hand, only had one parent. I personally think a child is a two-parent responsibility. It's not just about the parent. It's also what a child needs."

Silence descended over the room. Through the open window came the sounds of a few noisy insects and a bird scolding an intruder.

Griff grimaced as he adjusted his position on the big leather chair. "Some kids would be glad just to have one parent."

At the brooding in Griff's face, Maggie asked, "Are you speaking from experience?"

He shrugged.

It wasn't much of an answer. She decided to pursue her own curiosity. "Did you ever want kids?"

She didn't think he was going to answer at first. "Wanting and having are two different realities."

She noticed he didn't answer her question. Shadows crept across his face to shut out his thoughts. For some reason, she was reluctant to press him as to why. Instead she packed up the items she'd sewn and removed the sewing machine from the table.

Griff lumbered to his feet. "I'm going outside to get some fresh air. I'll be back shortly."

"Do you want some company?"

"No."

She watched him leave. He had to be in pain, but she noticed that he still refused to take any of the pain medication the doctor had prescribed. Nor did he complain about his injuries.

Her father had always said Griff was the toughest cop he'd ever known. She wondered if it was because of his past or because he was trying to prove himself.

She'd never heard either BJ or Griff talk about his family. Did he have brothers and sisters? Or was he an only child, like she had been?

She sensed the latter.

It took a lonely soul to recognize another one.

Griff would have tossed and turned on the lumpy sofa bed, but his cast made such a luxury impossible. He'd been able to do little more than doze since he'd finally managed to ease his frame into the bed. His leg had swollen, a result of all the strain he'd put on it throughout the day.

If that wasn't bad enough, he was also beset with erotic fantasies of tumbling Maggie into his bed and having hot and heavy sex.

What in the hell was the matter with him? He'd always kept a firm control over his hormones when it came to women.

Of course, Maggie wasn't just another woman. She was his wife. Maybe the fact that they were supposedly on their honeymoon was scrambling his head.

For the past hour, he'd made every attempt to divert his mind to the shooting. Or trying to identify the unfamiliar sounds of the northern Wisconsin night. Each endeavor met with futility.

Logically, he knew better than to get tangled up with someone like Maggie. For all of her arguments against getting married, she was a homebody. One only had to watch her tending to that pasty-faced doll she'd dragged out of her suitcase to realize how much she longed to be a mother. To have a family.

A man didn't fool around with a woman who made doll clothes.

Since Sonja's death, he'd always chosen safe women to date. Women who didn't want ties any more than he did. Women who walked away with no regrets.

In the dark night, Griff couldn't conjure a single face of any of those women. There hadn't been many of them. But there had been enough so that at least one of them should have made a lasting impression.

So why could he only see Maggie's freckled face in his mind's eye? Why did his fingertips tingle with the need to grab a fistful of her red hair and turn her mouth toward his?

The desire stirring in his loins was making his leg throb. He couldn't decide which was the greater pain.

Maggie knew Griff wasn't sleeping, either. She'd heard him shift on the couch, then turn on the light. Looking at the digital clock, she realized it was only five minutes later than the last time she'd looked.

She sat up and reached for her robe. There was no sense in trying to pretend either one of them could sleep. Before she opened the door, she pulled her suitcase from under the bed and retrieved the deck of cards she'd thrown in at the last minute.

Then she walked into the living room.

Griff didn't seem surprised to see her. He'd probably been as aware of her movements as she'd been of his. The small cabin didn't allow secrets.

She pulled a chair away from the table and sat down, propping the deck of cards in front of her. "Do you want to play gin rummy?"

He grimaced. "How many cards do you deal?"

"Ten. Match three of a kind or collect a run of three in the same suit."

He staggered to his feet. "Sounds easy enough."

When he tried to sit down, there was little room to put his stiff limb. Maggie jumped up and shoved the extra chair near him. Then she lifted his cast and propped it on several pillows. "That okay?" she asked.

"As good as it's going to get."

As Maggie dealt the first couple of hands, they didn't indulge in any chitchat.

The game was simple and easy to follow. Perhaps too easy, since Griff had plenty of time to watch the deft movement of Maggie's hands as she shuffled. Her fingers were strong, capable and utterly feminine. Just like the rest of her. Her just-out-of-bed mussed hair provided fertile ingredients to the fantasies he'd been weaving before she'd interrupted his musings.

When she drew a card from the discard pile and laid down a trio of tens, he thought of how it would feel to have those fingers raking his back in passion.

He'd never realized playing cards could be so erotic.

"Your turn," she said.

Their third game ended two plays later.

"Do you want something to drink?" she asked.

"What did you have in mind?"

"I make a mean hot root beer toddy. Can I tempt you?"

Oh, yeah. She tempted him all right. But he knew that she wasn't offering the kind of relief he desperately needed. Forcing his illicit thoughts to the back of his head, he said, "Make it a double."

"Whip cream or root beer?"

"Both."

"Coming right up."

Griff attempted to move his leg to a more comfortable position as Maggie opened the refrigerator.

"How's your leg feeling?" she asked.

"About the way I expected."

"That sofa bed can't be too comfortable."

"Are you volunteering to share yours?"

She stiffened and stopped pouring the root beer into a glass cup. Turning her head, she met his gaze. "I don't think that would be a good idea, do you?"

He sighed. "Sorry. I think this heat has gone to my brain."

She went back to her preparations. A minute later she set a steaming mug, topped with white foam, in front of him before putting one in front of her.

He took a sip. "Not bad."

"Wylie used to make these for me."

Griff watched Maggie lick the cream from her cup. Desire sliced through his gut. He gripped the mug in his hands and wondered how he was going to make it through the next night, and all the ones after that, and still keep his sanity. Making love to Maggie was becoming a dangerously obsessive thought.

"Do you want to play another round?" Maggie said, breaking the uncomfortable silence.

What he wanted he couldn't have.

She pushed back her chair. Before he could stop her, she touched the tense muscle in his uninjured leg and began to massage it.

"What are you—"

"Just sit back and relax," she said.

Relaxation was an impossibility. His leg muscle responded instantly to the caress of her fingers.

And so did his manhood.

Griff nearly groaned out loud. "Maggie—"

"You're so tense. It's no wonder you can't sleep."

She rotated her body so she could exert more pressure on his sore limb.

"Maggie." His voice sounded hoarse and unfamiliar.

She didn't seem to notice his sudden tension. "My friends said I should become a masseuse. I seem to have a natural ability to detect the pressure points that need be unlocked. You should feel better in a few minutes."

"Maggie, stop!" He all but shouted.

She lifted her hands and stared at him with wide eyes. "Did I hurt you?"

His gaze held hers. "That isn't the body part that's causing me the most trouble."

He lowered his gaze to his lap. When he glanced up again, he saw her eyes widen at his erection.

She swallowed and stepped carefully away from him. The refrigerator stopped her retreat.

"I guess the massage didn't work."

"It depends what muscle you were trying to assuage."

She jerkily reached for the deck of cards. "Do you want to play another hand of rummy?"

"Not unless you intend it to be foreplay."

The cards slipped from her hands and dropped to the floor.

Electrical awareness arced between them. Maggie didn't seem to breathe. The color faded from her cheeks.

"Maggie, go to bed," Griff ordered.

When had he started calling her Maggie instead of Bennington?

Why did it matter?

She swallowed the sudden lump in her throat. "I need to pick up the cards."

"Now, Maggie. Go now."

She paused only a half a second before she fled the room.

Griff exhaled slowly. It had been close. He didn't think he'd ever wanted a woman this much in his entire life. The scent of Maggie still lingered in his head.

If it was just about sex, maybe he'd have seduced her.

Maggie was a normal woman with normal needs surely. They could both scratch the itch that making love would relieve.

Yet, Griff's lust was tied up with images that weren't so lustful. Maggie fussing over her sewing. Wading into the water to free her fishing line. Shuffling the deck of cards. Propping his leg on a pillow. Nursing his tense tired muscle. God, he wanted something more than sex. She'd become far more hazardous to his health than the guy who'd fired a bullet into his leg.

Maggie Bennington was BJ's daughter. One didn't seduce a partner's daughter.

Griff had no business thinking what he was thinking.

That was the litany he repeated over and over the rest of the night.

Chapter 9

A gentle rain fell during the night but failed to dispel the unnatural heat and humidity. By the next morning the slick vegetation glistened with moisture, causing the mosquitoes to come out and feast.

Maggie considered trying her hand at fishing again, but the biting insects drove her back inside the cabin.

Griff's temper hadn't improved during the interim, either.

"Are you going to drag that damn sewing machine out again?"

She considered ignoring his crankiness. "You want to play cards?"

"For money or something more interesting?"

She refused to be baited. "I'll take that as a no."

Turning her back on him, she pulled her dress fabric and a spool of thread from the box and began to work.

Griff maneuvered his way to the end of the couch

and turned on the radio. He flipped through a variety of music stations before settling for a sports talk radio.

That lasted all of ten minutes. He raced through a host of programs, listening to one for a few minutes before moving to something else. The noise began to wear on Maggie's nerves. She had to bite her lip to keep from snapping at him to turn the radio off.

She realized that Griff didn't have as many choices as she did. Pursing her lips together, she did her best to block out the sound.

After thirty minutes of no talk and plenty of static, Maggie pushed aside the dress she'd hemmed.

"I'm going to drive into town to buy some mosquito spray and pick up a few other items."

Griff frowned. "That might not be a good idea."

"No one knows we're here. And if someone is looking for us, they'd assume we headed to Chicago or the Cities." He didn't seem convinced. "I'll wear a stocking cap to cover my hair. I can't stay in this cabin another minute."

"I'm coming with you."

Maggie wanted to protest but knew it was best if they stuck together.

Twenty minutes later they were en route to Jonas Falls.

Griff brought along his cell phone, and on the outskirts of town, his roam signal beamed on.

Maggie parked her station wagon in front of the small grocery store. "You coming in with me?"

Griff shook his head. "I'll try to raise Wylie on the phone."

Before he could place his call, the phone rang.

He flipped open the compact device. "Hello?"

Maggie started to open the car door but paused when Griff held up his hand to stop her.

"Hello?" he repeated.

"Who is it?"

He shook his head and spoke into the phone again. Finally he shut the phone.

"No one there?" she asked.

"There was someone on the other end. I could hear him breathing."

The phone trilled again. Griff waited a few seconds before speaking into the mouthpiece.

His expression became grimmer as he failed to raise a response from the person on the other end.

After he ended the connection, Maggie reached into the back and grabbed the Green Bay Packers stocking cap sitting behind her seat. She clamped it on her head. "How do I look?"

"Ready to tailgate."

"Good."

The phone rang again. This time they both ignored it.

"Be quick in there," Griff said.

She nodded and lifted the door latch.

Inside the store, she found the few items she needed.

The twenty-something salesclerk had a phone propped to her ear while she rang up Maggie's items and chewed gum at the same time.

The trip inside the store lasted less than three minutes.

When Maggie returned to the car, she heard Griff

talking on his phone. "When are you arriving here?" he asked the person on the other end.

He paused for a response, before saying, "Take the back roads. We've had a couple of 'out of area' phone calls. It might be a wrong number, or someone might be trying to track us down."

"Wylie?" Maggie mouthed to Griff.

He nodded before responding to the police sergeant. "Don't forget to bring those case files."

The call ended seconds later.

Maggie turned on the ignition. "When is Wylie planning to arrive?"

"Tonight."

"Has he learned anything?"

"No."

Much to Griff's relief, Wylie walked through the door shortly after eleven o'clock. He carried in a couple bags of groceries, and the large box of old case files Griff had requested.

Maggie had spent most of the evening down at the dock casting her fishing line. Griff hadn't bothered to join her. He sat at a small picnic table perched halfway between the lake and the cabin where he could keep her in sight.

They were getting on each other's nerves and desperately needed a respite.

After Wylie unloaded his gifts, he joined Maggie at the table.

He eyed her strained features and Griff's whiskered face. Griff hadn't asked her to help him shave that morning and she didn't volunteer.

"You two look like you haven't slept since you got here," the older man observed.

"Can you contact the doctor and see about my getting out of the monkey harness?"

Wylie nodded. "I'll see what I can do."

"What kind of leads are you following?" Maggie asked.

Wylie stood up and walked to the refrigerator. He grabbed a soda and drank half of it before reclaiming his place near Maggie. "The thieves had a storage locker at the bus depot. Myers and Karns went through and found quite a stash of goods. Most of them were items that had been reported missing from several large weddings. They also had a cache of credit cards."

"Any guns or ammunition?" Griff asked. He'd decided to stay on the couch. Despite Wylie's presence, he was conscious of Maggie's every move. The old flannel shirt and sweatpants she wore should have been a turnoff. For some reason, his body wasn't receiving that message. In his opinion, she looked damn near good enough to eat.

Wylie threw his empty can in the recyclable bin. "No guns. No bullets. We've checked and rechecked the reports on the other wedding heists. No one reported seeing or hearing guns being fired."

"You don't think the thieves were behind the shooting."

Wylie shook his head. "Anything is possible, but I don't know why someone would shoot you after we had their comrades in handcuffs. They didn't take a shot at the arresting officers. Why one of you? He had nothing to gain.''

''What else do we have?''

''I've been following up on your recent arrests. So far everyone has alibis.''

''What about the Williams brothers?''

''They're both in lock-up. They were hauled in for a barroom brawl three weeks ago, and the judge revoked their parole. They'll be eating state food for the next two years at a minimum.''

The Williams brothers were at the top of Griff's list of possible suspects. He had reviewed all his cases over the past week. He'd had several people threaten him throughout the course of his career. But most of them had been drunk and probably didn't even remember his name.

''Maggie, have you heard from Dwight Conrad recently?''

Wylie's unexpected question brought Griff's head up.

Maggie turned away but not before he witnessed the tight freezing in her expression.

What did Dwight Conrad have to do with Maggie?

The former Pendleton officer had abruptly handed in his resignation from the department about the same time as Maggie.

''I don't know where he is. And I don't care to know where he is,'' Maggie said. ''Why?''

''He checked out of a drug rehab center, and no one has seen him since.''

''What has he got to do with this?'' Griff asked tersely.

''Nothing,'' came Maggie's short response.

Griff caught the warning look she flashed Wylie. Whatever relationship Conrad had with her, she didn't want shared.

Wylie's expression was troubled, but he didn't offer any insights into why the former officer was a possible suspect.

Conrad had never been one of Griff's favorite people. He'd joined the department shortly after Griff. But while Griff had earned his stripes, Conrad had tried to take shortcuts. In the end, he lost whatever ground he tried to gain. He wasn't known to be a team player, and few in the department liked him as a partner.

''His drug rehab was court-ordered?'' Griff asked.

''Yeah.'' Wylie grimaced.

No other information was forthcoming from either Maggie or Wylie. Griff was left to re-cap his own few memories of Conrad's departure, and realized he had little to none. BJ had been as closemouthed about Conrad's resignation as he had about Maggie's.

What had Maggie's sudden leaving had to do with Conrad? Or vice versa?

For the second time in the past few days, Griff questioned the events of three years ago. Why had Maggie really left?

Why hadn't BJ tried to stop her?

And how did Conrad fit into the picture? There didn't seem to be any common thread that Griff could detect.

From Maggie's militantly closed expression, Griff knew he wasn't going to find any easy answers.

Wylie stayed another hour. Before he left, Maggie excused herself and escaped behind the bedroom door.

Wylie turned to Griff before he stepped into the night. "How are you two getting along?"

"We've locked up the ammunition."

The older man seemed to have something on his mind. "Don't be too hard on her. She didn't have to agree to this."

There was little Griff could say.

Wylie started to turn away and then stopped. "By the way, your landlady has called a couple of times requesting a forwarding address for your mail."

"Why doesn't she just drop it at the department?"

Wylie rolled his eyes. "She claims she doesn't want to be responsible if we lose it."

Griff chuckled. "Just tell her to hold on to it and I'll collect it later."

Wylie saluted and headed into the night.

He watched the rear lights of his police sergeant's car until they faded into the night.

Inside, the door between him and Maggie was a formidable barrier. He hobbled back toward his lonely bed.

By all indications, it was going to be another long night. He doubted if Maggie would come out and play gin rummy with him.

A crashing thunderstorm shook the tiny house two hours later. A blinding flash of lightning lit up the entire cabin before a cupboard-rattling boom.

Suddenly the electricity went off. Except for the illuminated digital numbers from the clock near the sofa bed, the only light that had been on was a small night-light located in the kitchen. The room pitched into total darkness.

Griff groped for his crutch before finding his footing. He remembered seeing a flashlight in the drawer next to the sink.

He began to inch across the room as another boom of thunder erupted.

Just then the bedroom door flew open and before he could brace himself, Maggie ran full barrel into his chest.

The force of her body caught him off-guard. His crutch crashed to the floor as his arms came around her. The momentum carried them both into the couch.

Before he could catch his breath, Maggie was pounding against his chest. "Get off me!" she yelled.

"Whoa! You're the one who ran into me."

She didn't seem to hear him. Her body twisted. Her knee just missed a strategic part of his body.

"Maggie."

"Get off. I said get off." She sounded hysterical.

He grabbed her arms and held her still. "Maggie, just hold on. Give me a second, and I'll get my balance."

She was amazingly strong.

The lights flickered. He saw her wide-eyed terror in the split second before they went out again. Even though the electricity had only resumed for a brief moment, it was enough for Maggie to see his face. She went still beneath him.

Not taking any chances, he levered his body off hers and stood up.

Breathing heavily, he said. "Stay there. I know where the flashlights and candles are."

She didn't answer him. The ragged edges of her breathing were tinged with a slight whimper. He couldn't quite match the woman who'd been his mainstay in the ambulance and had waded into unfamiliar water with the terrified one who was determined to be victorious over her fears.

He had to raise his voice to be heard over the raging storm. Yet he tried to make it soothing and monotone.

"Here's the drawer." He fumbled around. "Found the flashlight. Let's pray the batteries are charged."

Fortunately they were. As soon as he pressed the button, a narrow stream of light flooded the kitchen area. "Now let's see if there's any matches. Hey, even better, a lighter."

He lit the two candles he'd found. Dragging his injured leg, he managed to place one lit candle on the counter before bringing the other one to the end table next to the couch.

The wavery light illuminated Maggie's pinched features. Some of the terror had faded from her face but not entirely. Her shoulders shivered.

Griff found the crutch he'd dropped and propelled himself toward the bedroom. He snagged the comforter from the bed and returned to Maggie.

Gently wrapping the bedding around her, he sat down next to her on the sofa bed. "Doozy of a storm, isn't it? Must have a major cold front swooping down from the Arctic colliding head-on with that Gulf Stream warm front. Could get some hail—"

His words were drowned out by a noise that

sounded like millions of pebbles pounding against the windows and roof.

Maggie's head pressed into his shoulder, her body shaking rivaled the rattling of the windows.

Griff kept talking about clouds, weather patterns and seasonal transitions, not hearing the words he spoke. He just wanted to drown out the noise and still the shivering woman in his arms.

He'd never been known for his bedside manner. If anything, he tended to be too brusque and overbearing. But that's not what Maggie needed. He listened to his gut and kept a steady recitation.

The woman in his arms pressed closer to him. He responded by pulling her tighter to him.

As quickly as the storm came up, it died away. When the last ping of rain hit the window pane, Maggie turned her face from his sleeve and leaned against him with a heavy sigh.

"Glad that's over. It sounded like we were in a popcorn popper," Griff commented dryly.

Maggie sat up, separating herself from him, and Griff's arms felt strangely bereft at her withdrawal.

She managed to produce a self-conscious laugh. "You must think I'm a sap."

He shook his head. "Saps don't aim strong right hooks at their comforters."

Her gaze darted toward him and then away again. "Is that what you were trying to do? Comfort me?"

It was a good thing it was dark, and she couldn't see the flush working its way across his jawbone. "Not much good at it, am I?"

She surprised him by reaching over and squeezing his good hand. "It worked for me."

She released his hand and abruptly dashed the tears with the back of her hand. "The electricity didn't come back on."

"I should check the breaker. The switch might have popped."

He didn't move, however.

Griff had to struggle not to pull Maggie back into his arms.

What would she do if he did?

Holding her had ignited the sexual hungers that had been tormenting him since they'd arrived. Oddly, he hadn't been thinking about sex when he'd held her. He'd only wanted to soothe her fears.

Now he wanted something to reaffirm the feelings tossing inside him. He wanted to stake a physical claim.

It was only through sheer force that he kept from acting out his sudden need.

Thankfully, Maggie slid to the end of the bed and stood up. She walked across the room and peered out the window. "Why do you know so much about the weather?"

Her attempt at a neutral subject made him frown. Had he been the only one to notice the sensual tug of war between them?

He wanted her to…

To what? Leap back into his arms so they could make passionate love?

Hell yes. That's exactly what he wanted. Exactly what he didn't need.

Even in the dimly lit room he could see the outline of Maggie's rigid back.

Maggie had been smart to pull away.

He leaned back against the sofa and clasped his good hand behind his head and forced himself to contemplate her question. "One of my foster fathers was a weatherman," he said. "I wanted to be just like him, so I learned everything I could to impress him. Now it's sort of a hobby."

Maggie turned toward him. "You were in a foster home?"

"I lived with seven different foster families."

She returned to the edge of the bed. "What happened to your real family?"

The tension that had tormented him a few minutes earlier shifted.

Griff didn't like talking about his childhood. But he was the one who had opened this door. He lowered his hand. "I never knew my dad. My mom and I moved around a lot until I was five years old. A social worker showed up one day and insisted I go to school. When I arrived home, my mother was gone. I lived on my own for a week before anyone noticed. From then on, I was shuffled from place to place."

Maggie sat down next to his plastered leg. All the terror had evaporated from her face. "You never had a real home of your own."

Telling her about his childhood wasn't as difficult as he feared. "I learned to live light and to always keep a suitcase handy. BJ was the only person who never walked away."

Guilt niggled at Maggie. "I'm sorry."

"For what? You weren't the one who walked out the door."

"I hated you and begrudged you Dad's friendship."

"If BJ had been my father, I would have reacted the same way you did. I was a convenient target."

"That doesn't excuse bad behavior. My problems with Dad weren't your fault. I had no right to blame you for something that never had a thing to do with you."

"What caused your nightmare, Maggie?" he asked.

His change of subject brought Maggie up short. She looked down at her fingers, which had coiled into fists. "I don't remember. It was a bad dream."

"Did it have anything to do with Dwight Conrad?"

"No. Of course not."

"Then what?"

She shook her head. "It's nothing. Let's just forget it."

"Hey, you owe me something."

"What?"

"I told you about my murky past."

He made the words light but Maggie knew that he hadn't wanted to tell her about his mother. What person wanted to admit he'd been abandoned? Griff would never want to sound weak or needy.

She found herself pulled. Part of her wanted to continue to keep her secrets to herself. The other part wanted to share the burdens she'd shouldered for as long as she could remember. Her inner skirmish was short-lived. Griff's pain was every bit as wounding as hers.

She swallowed, pushing back her fear of being vulnerable to this man. "I've been afraid of storms ever since I was eight years old."

"What happened when you were eight?"

"Dad was on duty. I usually stayed at the neighbor's while he was working. One day the neighbor's mother got sick and was rushed to the hospital. Since it was only a half an hour before my dad was to come home, I said I could stay home by myself. She called Dad to tell him. But before he arrived, a tornado ripped through the neighborhood and wiped out two houses next to ours." Maggie's arms enclosed her midsection as she recalled her fear and the awful howl of the wind.

"You weren't hurt?"

"Not in any way you could see. But I'm the biggest baby whenever there's a storm. Dad couldn't understand it."

The slight catch in Maggie's voice made Griff flinch. He hated ripping the scabs from her scars. "Your dad loved you more than life itself."

"I just wish that could have been enough." She lifted her chin, as if trying to shake off her sudden depression. "You said you know something about circuit breakers."

She'd given them the perfect opportunity to move on. Griff considered her clenched hands.

He couldn't allow it. He had to break down the barrier she had erected, even though he, of all people, knew how important it was for her to be strong and keep in control.

The temptation to let her keep her secrets was stronger than it should have been. Griff forced himself to keep on task and press for the answers he needed. "What about Conrad, Maggie? Why did Wylie ask you about him?"

"Dwight Conrad has nothing to do with this."

"We don't know anything for sure. If there's even a small chance that he shot me, then I need to know."

Maggie looked poised ready to flee. Griff saw the struggle of uncertainty on her face.

"He left a week after you resigned," he prodded.

"Yes." Her clipped answer was meant to discourage his invasion into her life.

"Why?"

"Wylie and Dad arranged it."

Getting answers from Maggie was like pulling teeth. He searched for a different tact. "Didn't you and Dwight date?"

An intense fury flashed across Maggie's face. "No. Never."

"But he asked."

"Yes. Then he didn't bother asking. He tried to blackmail me into going out with him."

"He sexually harassed you?"

"You don't believe me."

It wasn't a question, Griff realized. She didn't expect him to believe her.

Suddenly the puzzle pieces tumbled into place. She hadn't turned her back on either her job or her dad. If anything, it was just the opposite. In her mind her job and her dad had let her down. She'd felt betrayed.

Her stiff posture told Griff she was bracing for his condemnation, as well.

"I believe you," he said, letting his unflinching gaze punctuate his surety.

Without waiting for her reaction, he reached for his crutch. It was time to give them both a break. "Where's the fuse box?"

She pointed to the other room. "Inside the closet near the kitchen."

Griff pocketed the flashlight and limped across the floor. Swinging open the metal box, he found the switches.

Within seconds, the night-light and clock came on. He shut the door and returned to the sofa bed. Maggie was sitting on the edge.

"Why do you believe me?" she asked.

Griff reclaimed his position next to her and propped his cast. "Conrad was always a sleaze. He thought his oily charm made him the answer to any woman's dreams."

"Dad didn't believe me."

"What makes you say that?"

"I wanted to press charges, but Dad told me that it would be hard to prove. I could tell he was angry at me for letting this happen, implying that I was responsible in some way. So I resigned." She stood up, as if she couldn't sit still any longer. "I finally realized that my father was never going to be the dad I needed. He was a cop. That's what he knew and was good at. I was just in the way. So I handed in my notice and left." She reached up and rubbed her temples. "I wasted so much of my time trying to be the daughter he wanted."

Once again the urge to haul Maggie into his arms

swept through Griff. He wished BJ had told him about the harassment. Griff wouldn't have let Conrad slink off without a good beating. It was nothing less than he deserved.

"Your father was trying to protect you."

"Was he? I don't think so. How would it look if his only child brought out the department's ugly little secret?" She waved her hand dismissively. "It was better to sweep it under the rug and pretend it never happened."

"If BJ and Wylie made Conrad resign, then they believed you and refused to hide anything."

"Conrad should have been judged by the courts."

"And so would you have been."

"I was willing to take that chance."

Griff understood BJ's dilemma. "But your dad wasn't. We all know how the system works. Defense attorneys are notorious for putting the victims on trial. Knowing your dad's temper, Wylie probably had to physically restrain him from beating the crap out of that slimy Conrad. They would have had to answer to the law. However, they could strong-arm him into forcing his resignation. In doing that, they took action but protected you."

"It should have been my decision to make. It's our job to hold lawbreakers accountable."

"You're right. But Conrad would have found a lowlife defense attorney who wouldn't be afraid to cast innuendoes and rip your character to shreds. Your dad wasn't willing to let that happen. He acted like a father, not a police officer."

Griff could feel the rage and hurt churn within Maggie, even though she kept her feelings buried.

A tear slipped down her cheek.

Griff attempted to do everything in his power to stay where he was.

Maggie was BJ's daughter.

She hated his guts.

The last person in the world she would want to lean on was Griff.

Touching her could mean lighting a fuse to his raging hormones.

Each argument was sound. He should listen to his common sense.

Instead he heeded the nagging in his gut and reached for her.

Her body went taut.

"Don't—"

He ignored her protests and pressed her face into his shoulder. "Don't think for now."

She stubbornly lifted her head. "But—"

He sighed and gently pushed her head down again. "Nothing is going to happen. I've got my leg in a cast. You might as well take advantage of my weakness, Maggie. You're never going to get another chance."

Chapter 10

Maggie didn't relax right away.

She was used to taking care of herself. Griff understood that. He also knew that there was no way he was going to let her ride this storm out by herself.

Finally the rigidity left her body and her limbs melted into his.

"Anybody who believes you're weak is a fool," she said, disputing his claim of weakness.

A thin smile tugged at his mouth. "I have to be strong if I'm going to be married to you."

He felt her silent chuckle. "Lucky for you it's not a life sentence."

Yeah. He should have felt lucky.

He didn't.

As she cuddled closer, his body battled its own tension and he hoped she didn't notice the telltale bulge beneath his jeans. There wasn't an ounce of truth that his actions were platonic or that he was weak. He'd need to be unconscious not to be aware of the woman in his arms.

And it had nothing to do with the fact that she was BJ's daughter or that he was under some kind of macho creed to protect her.

The truth was that he wanted Maggie Bennington in the basic way a man wants a woman.

He wanted to see her use the incredible feminine power she'd used to conquer her fears to strip naked and wrap herself around him. The itch that had begun at the church had burgeoned beyond sex. He wanted to hear her whisper his name. He wanted to hear her every thought.

When had he ever wanted more than light conversation from a member of the opposite sex?

It wasn't that he didn't respect women. He'd worked well with female officers. They brought unique perspectives to investigations.

Yet it had been a long time since he'd wanted to share any part of his life with one. Not since Sonja.

With Maggie curled into his arms and the night hours ticking slowly away, Griff tried to recall the face of his late wife in his mind.

Sonja.

She'd been his wife. He'd trusted her. And she'd betrayed him.

Maggie shifted and her arm slipped trustingly to his waist.

Mother of God. He'd never endured such torture.

How could he use the hard lessons from his past as

armor against the silk of Maggie's hair caressing his jaw line? He liked feeling her in his arms.

Even though the storm had long died away, he throbbed with a protectiveness that made him yearn to stay in this position for the rest of the night and beyond.

With the rhythm of Griff's heart resounding in Maggie's ear, she couldn't believe she was leaning on the man who had made her life miserable for years. It was the last position she'd ever wanted to find herself in.

Griff was her nemesis.

He'd taken her place in her father's life.

Yet she had absolutely no desire to move. She wasn't a prisoner. She'd have thrown Griff off her if he'd even tried to pin her down.

Her father was long gone.

And she wanted to be here.

It had been a long time, if ever, since she'd felt so safe.

What a pair they were. Griff anchored down by a cast. She tormented by her childish fears of storms.

So why did she suspect if the wind and rain returned, she wouldn't even flinch?

Because she was finding security where she'd never expected to find it.

She'd seen the anger in Griff's face when she'd told him about Dwight Conrad's actions. She'd worry for the weaker man if their paths ever crossed again. The former officer was cowardly. He tried to use intimidation to coerce women into going out with him.

What Griff didn't realize was that Dwight had never been a danger to her. Not in the way Griff could be.

Griff had an internal strength that would never be used against another person unless he or she invited it.

He'd be easy for a lesser person to lean upon. That knowledge alone should have made her ease away and put some distance between them.

But Maggie didn't move. She wanted to be here in his arms. He made her feel incredibly feminine and cherished.

It was a heady, sexy experience.

She'd never been so threatened in her life.

Like a turned on water faucet, the rain returned the next morning, forcing Maggie to stay indoors with Griff.

From the moment Maggie had wakened in Griff's arms, the edginess had resurfaced and sharpened between them.

In the light of day, she couldn't hide from the truths of her momentary lapse during the nighttime darkness. Griff didn't question her sudden coolness.

He seemed burdened by his own thoughts, a perpetual frown adorning his closed features.

After he'd emerged from the bathroom, she noticed he had done his own shaving. She chose not to comment on the few nicks decorating his jaw. They both needed to keep a respectful space.

Griff pulled the box of files over to the sofa and checked through the contents while she repositioned her sewing machine on the table. For the first hour, neither of them spoke while the rain kept a steady beat.

She'd just finished making a small choker for one of her dolls when Griff pushed aside the files.

She raised her head. "No luck?"

"Do you remember the schoolteacher case?"

She removed the pins from her mouth. "Yep. A forty-something school teacher accused of seducing one of his students. The girl's parents wanted to press charges, but she refused to cooperate until he went back to his wife."

"What happened?"

"The teacher agreed to a plea bargain. He provided some information about another member of the staff who was involved in drug trafficking. The teacher got probation but lost his job."

"It says here that he made threats against the girl and you."

She shook her head. "His wife left him. He wanted someone to blame, and I was handy."

"Where is he now?"

"He moved out of town."

Griff watched as Maggie leaned over to retrieve a pattern for a long skirt.

He had fight to keep his mind on the case file in front of him.

"What about the girl?"

Maggie lifted an eyebrow. "She graduated from high school and got herself pregnant a year later."

"When did you start collecting dolls?"

His change of subject startled Maggie, causing her to nearly stab her finger with a pin. She grimaced, shaking her hand. "Aunt Jessica bought me a doll after each one of her trips."

"When did they become more than a gift?"

She picked up the dress and held it against the doll she'd managed to find space for in her suitcase. "Dad was gone so much. The dolls were always there. They became a part of the family."

Griff seemed inordinately curious. "BJ never mentioned your fondness for dolls."

"Dad had little patience with Aunt Jessica's attempt to feminize me. Whenever one of the dolls arrived, Dad would sulk."

"He was jealous."

Maggie eyed him suspiciously. "Why would he be jealous or threatened by his own sister?"

"You were a girl. She's a woman. The female sex wasn't BJ's strong suit."

She set down the doll and pushed aside her sewing. "Or yours, either. Right?"

He was suddenly on guard. "What does that mean?"

"Maybe you're right. Dad was jealous, and instead of spending more time with me, building a bond between us, he pulled away. But what about you? Aren't you doing the same thing? Isn't that why you're the great expert?"

"This isn't about me."

She tilted her head. "It's easier to stand on the sidelines and judge someone else's life, isn't it? You don't put yourself at risk."

An all-too-familiar shutter descended over Griff's

expression, shutting Maggie out of his thoughts. He'd gone into hiding, just like her father used to.

Her father's jealousies didn't hurt her nearly as much as she thought they might.

What bothered her more was the unmasking of her emotions in front of Griff.

Raw and exposed, the walls in the cabin suddenly crowded her.

She stood up. "I need to get out of here, rain or no rain."

Griff grasped the crutch leaning against the wall. "We should drive into town and give Wylie a call. He told us to check in."

Maggie would have preferred going by herself.

Like it or not, she didn't have a choice.

Any further personal subjects were shelved as they wove down the tiny lane and hit the main highway twenty minutes later.

That was fine with Griff. Griff didn't want to analyze the hidden truths behind Maggie's relationship with her father or his own character flaws.

Maggie was right. He much preferred analyzing other people's problems than his own. That's probably why he'd become a cop. Society's dysfunctionalism could take front and center. The code of professionalism became a protective shield.

So how had the conversation turned back to him?

He'd always suspected BJ's relationship with Maggie had been determined by his partner's insecurities as a parent.

There was no reason why Griff had this intense need to explain or defend BJ's actions.

Why did Griff care about something that no longer mattered?

Because you're starting to care more about Maggie than you should.

She was BJ's daughter. Of course he'd care.

Is that the truth, or are you trying to hide behind your badge and the job, as Maggie accused?

His mouth pressed into a flat line of denial as the question about-faced and shot back at him.

Had Maggie been right? Was he standing on the sidelines? Was he really trying to cover his own flank?

He'd always prided himself on his honesty, but maybe the truths of his life were based on dishonesty.

The skin beneath the plaster started to itch.

"Is your phone working yet?" Maggie's words broke into his mental interrogation as they broached the town limits.

Griff reached into his shirt pocket and turned on the phone. "It's on."

Wylie answered on the third ring. The terseness in the older man's tone came through loud and clear. "Where are you?" Wylie asked.

"We're on the outskirts of Jonas Falls. What's up?"

"Local mail carrier was mugged two hours ago."

"Is he okay?"

"It's a woman. She's still unconscious. I'm at the hospital right now."

Muggings weren't common in Pendleton, but they

weren't unheard of either. "Any possible clues as to why she'd be a target?"

"Today she was distributing local phone bills. Her mail bag is missing."

"What route does she cover?"

There was a brief hesitation. "Mine."

Griff's gut clenched. "You think someone might be tracking your phone calls to find us?"

"It's a stretch, but nothing in this case has made any sense. And there's something else you should know."

"What's that?"

Maggie pulled the car into a nearly vacant parking lot and turned to watch him.

"Dwight Conrad showed up this morning," Wylie said.

"Where?"

"Here at the department."

Griff clutched the phone. "What did he want?"

"His old job back."

Before Griff could question him, he heard Wylie speak in a muffled tone to someone else.

"Sorry about that. Where was I?"

"Conrad wants his old job back," Griff repeated. "Did you ask him where he's been?"

"Yeah. He said he'd been visiting his girlfriend in Chicago."

"Did you check it out?"

"Haven't had time. We got the call about the mugging. Conrad disappeared before I returned from the hospital."

There was another interruption in the background.

Thirty seconds later, Wylie returned. "Man, that woman's a pest."

"Who?"

"Mrs. Harris, your landlady. She claims she's being harassed by your bill collectors because you skipped town."

"Do you want me to talk to her?"

"No, we've got it covered," Wylie said. "Look, I've got to go. I want you two to sit tight at the cabin. I'll get word to you as soon as I've got something for you."

After he terminated the connection, Griff filled Maggie in about Dwight Conrad and the postwoman's mugging.

Maggie chewed on the corner of her lip and contemplated the street in front of them. "Would Dwight show up at the police department after he knocked out the maillady?"

"Maybe he was trying to establish an alibi."

"When was she attacked?"

"No one knows for sure. They figure she was at least an hour behind her route when they found her." Griff tried to move his leg. He'd pushed the seat back as far as it would allow. There still wasn't any room, but he hated riding in the back seat. Being a passenger was hard enough.

"Conrad's too much of a coward to boldly walk into the station after he knocked someone on the head," Maggie said.

"He wants his job back. Maybe this was the plan all along. First he tries to get rid of you so there's no reason why he can't return."

"And when that didn't work, he tried to find me through the phone billings. Afterward he attempts to cover his tracks by being at the police department when she's found." Maggie shook her head. "I still can't see it."

"Wylie wants us to stick as close to the cabin as possible. We'd better head back."

Maggie hit the steering wheel with the palm of her hand. "I feel like we're sitting ducks."

She had Griff's full agreement. He wanted nothing more than to confront their tormentor face-to-face. If it were just him, he wouldn't be cowering in the north woods. But there was still Maggie. She'd be out in the open if they went back.

For now, they'd have to sit tight.

Griff removed his sling after they returned to the apartment. Maggie had argued against it, but he insisted his arm would heal faster if the blood was free to circulate without being locked into place.

Two hours later, as Maggie started preparing macaroni and cheese for their dinner, a knock sounded on the outside door.

"Maggie, don't—" Griff's words were brought to a halt as she cautiously cracked open the door.

He saw the color drain from her face. "What are you doing here?"

Griff picked up his gun and pushed her aside to face their uninvited visitor.

His gaze narrowed at the sight of Dwight Conrad standing on the front stoop. "Conrad. What are you doing here?"

No wonder Wylie hadn't been able to track down the former officer. He must have hightailed it out of town as soon as he'd left the department.

"Hi, Murdock. I'd heard you two got married." Dwight's eyes shifted between Maggie and Griff. He thrust out his hand. "Congratulations."

Griff ignored the outstretched hand. From what he could tell, Conrad wasn't packing a firearm beneath his long-sleeved T-shirt and khaki pants. That didn't mean he wouldn't try to pull something. "What do you want?"

Conrad lowered his arm. "Man, this is awkward, isn't it? With you on your honeymoon and all. But I need to talk to Maggie. Do you mind if I come in?"

"Yes, we do mind. We're on our honeymoon." Griff wasn't inclined to be remotely friendly or social. "How did you find us?"

"I made a few calls. This place is listed in Wylie's sister's name. I met her husband once. The rest was easy."

Maggie ducked under the arm Griff had used to block the doorway, brushing aside his bodily attempt to shield her. "What's so important that you had to knock out a postal carrier?"

Dwight blanched. "You don't think I had anything to do with that, do you? Why would I?"

"You tell us," Griff demanded, not hiding his contempt of his former peer.

The other man stood a good three inches shorter than Griff. He'd permed his hair in an attempt to cover his rapidly balding head. There was little about the man Griff liked, especially his futile effort to look younger than he was. Conrad would always try to be something he wasn't.

When Griff refused to budge from the doorway, Dwight had the gall to wink at him. "I understand. You two want to be alone."

Griff's patience had run out. He grabbed Maggie's arm and started to pull her into the room. "Goodbye, Conrad."

"No. Wait." The other man put out a hand. "Maggie, I need your help."

Maggie pulled her arm free from Griff's grasp. She glared at him before turning her attention back to the former officer and her harasser. "What do you want, Dwight?"

"I want you to put in a good word for me with Wylie. I need my old job back. I know we had a serious misunderstanding—"

"You tried to coerce me into sleeping with you."

From the expression on Conrad's face, he looked ready to argue. But he stopped when he realized Maggie was turning away from him. "You're right. What I did was wrong, and I have no right to ask for your forgiveness. But my girlfriend is pregnant, and I need my old job."

Before Maggie could answer, Griff interrupted, "Did you try to take out Maggie at the wedding?"

"No. Never." Conrad's vehemence rang truer than anything else he'd said so far.

Maggie glanced at Griff. His expression remained stone cold.

She once again eyed the balding man on their doorstep. There was nothing Dwight Conrad could do or say that would make her like him. He would always be the kind of person who would try to slide through the cracks without paying his due. But she didn't wish him ill. He just wasn't worth her anger or her contempt for that matter.

"Why should Maggie put in a good word for you?" Griff asked.

"Because she's a woman. Women like babies," he blurted out. "And my baby is going to need a father who can afford to feed it."

Maggie almost smiled. The weasel didn't have a clue about how to be politically correct.

He was right about one thing. She couldn't hurt a child. But neither did she believe the Pendleton Police Department deserved having him back in their ranks.

"I won't intercede on your behalf at the department," she said, "but I'll ask Wylie to give you a character reference for a job somewhere else."

Before he could speak, she held out her hand to stop him. "There's one stipulation."

"What's that?"

"You have to finish your drug treatment program. Your child deserves a drug-free parent."

His gaze shifted away. "Yeah, I suppose you're right."

Griff, who had held his peace until now, added, "You also keep your mouth shut about this place or seeing us. If you don't, all bets are off."

Dwight gave a jaunty salute, spun around and left quickly.

Maggie watched him go. "That poor baby."

Griff pulled her back into the cabin and locked the

door. "He's right, you're too soft for your own good. He knew he could manipulate you."

"Are you telling me you don't feel sorry for an innocent child?" Maggie tugged free from his grasp. "Compassion isn't a sign of softness."

"Did you ever consider Conrad might not be on the level? He might not have a pregnant girlfriend."

"I considered it. Then I decided it didn't matter. I don't want him coming back."

"You don't think he took a shot at us?"

"No, do you?"

Griff reached into the cupboard and retrieved his holster for the gun. "I don't think he's a good enough shot to have nailed me on that church step. But let's follow him to make sure he's not doubling back."

"Shouldn't we contact Wylie?"

"We'll give him a call as soon we're sure where our rodent is headed."

Chapter 11

Dwight Conrad barely slowed down for the Jonas Falls city limits before catching the interstate south. There was no hint that he would make back to the cabin.

Griff made the phone call to Wylie as Maggie made a U-turn with the station wagon.

As soon as the older man answered, Griff filled him in on the recent events.

"You think he's headed back here?" Wylie asked.

"If he wants a reference, he will."

"Fine. I'll handle things on this end. In the meantime, maybe you and Maggie should leave the cabin and find another location."

Griff frowned. He lowered the phone and eyed Maggie's remote face. "Wylie thinks we should leave the cabin."

She shook her head. "No. Running didn't work the first time. If he tracks us here, then we'll be waiting for him."

Griff gave her a grim smile and restored the receiver to his ear. "We're staying."

Wylie didn't sound pleased, but he didn't argue, either. He promised to contact the local authorities in case Conrad returned to the area.

Without another word, they drove back to the cabin to finish fixing the dinner they'd hastily abandoned.

After Maggie cleaned up the dishes, she crossed the floor to where Griff lounged in the big leather chair, his leg draped across the hassock, studying another group of files.

She peered over his shoulder and scanned the file he held.

"That's one of Dad's old cases."

"BJ made more than a few enemies. Maybe one of them is the person who shot me and knocked out the mail carrier."

"Any luck?"

"Maybe. Take a look at this one."

She sat down on the couch across from him and pulled the pages toward her. "Joe Flint? That name sounds familiar."

"It was a case that BJ worked with another officer while I took a sabbatical one summer to attend classes. I never met Flint, but the man was a real lowlife."

Maggie skimmed through the report. "He was found guilty of abusing and killing his stepson."

"Your dad was the key witness."

"Where's Flint now?"

"He was released from prison a month ago."

Maggie pushed aside the report. "But you didn't have anything to do with the case. And this happened several years before I joined the department."

Griff posed his elbows on the armrest of the chair, steepling his fingers. "It wouldn't be the first time someone transferred their hate for one individual to another. With BJ gone, we'd be the likely targets."

She flipped through the case file again and pulled out the mug shot of Joe Flint. "His hair was pretty thin in this picture. He's probably bald by now."

"Which doesn't help us much if he's wearing a hair piece or a cap."

Maggie couldn't stand feeling so inactive. She stood up and paced the small length of the room. "We'll need to have Wylie check on this."

Griff grimaced and lowered his hands. "We could probably create a scenario from each of these files."

She poked at a file sitting off to the side. "What about this one?"

"Dead. Frank Rankin committed suicide."

She slumped in her chair and sighed. "I hate feeling like we're pigeons waiting to be plucked."

"It's our best bet for flushing this guy out." He met her gaze over the tips of his fingers. "We sit tight and keep an eye on each other's backsides."

Had she just imagined it, or was there a definitive edge to Griff's voice?

His eyes seemed more secretive than usual, glistening with a palpitating intensity. He'd become a cop again, remote and separate. She recognized the signs.

Maggie tried to convince herself that she was overly sensitive to the barometric changes inside the four walls because of the storm the night before. Maybe she was just tired and imagining things she had no business imagining.

"I need to get some sleep," she said, heading toward the bedroom.

Guilt stopped her short. She turned and looked back at the man watching her. "Is there anything you need?"

Griff didn't answer for a long moment. "No, there's nothing that I need."

She hesitated, then shut the door. It was best for them both if they continued to ignore the spiraling sexual undercurrents.

No storm rocked or rattled the small house during the night. Nevertheless, Maggie awakened frequently.

She tried to reexamine the facts of the shooting to find a missing clue. But her mind seemed to slip a cog every time she reviewed the wedding. Her ears zeroed in on any sound coming from the other room.

Was Griff sleeping?

How did he sleep? On his side? His back?

Did he usually toss and turn or did he sleep like the dead?

She suspected he slept with one eye open, even on normal nights.

Was he ever not a cop?

She couldn't imagine him doing anything else. He had a built-in radar.

Maggie's curiosity took a forbidden turn. What was Griff like as a lover? As a husband?

Maggie, you're trespassing into dangerous waters again.

The admonition did little to dampen her fertile imagination.

Griff stared at the closed door and made a stab at telling himself it was for the best that it stayed that way.

They didn't need to add any more complications to this situation than were already there.

For the first time in his life, he was having trouble keeping his mind on his job. Even with Sonja, he had been more devoted to his partner and the department than to his wife. That had been her biggest complaint.

He didn't remember his mind suddenly spiraling off into illicit directions when he was investigating homicides, carjackings or robberies. The job had always risen to the top.

Yet tonight he'd been dangerously close to losing complete control. He'd wanted Maggie and to hell with the consequences.

She wore a long-tailed shirt with faded jeans. There was nothing the least bit sexy about her clothes, so why did he want to strip away each piece of clothing and take her right there on the hard floor?

Even the thick wool socks on her feet held his fascination.

Griff tried to slap some sense into his lust-driven thoughts.

He should be considering the next move of the would-be murderer. That would be the obvious channel to explore.

Maggie made him want to analyze the tantalizing smoothness of her hair, delve into the secrets behind her lips and investigate her innate softness.

He'd never believed softness was a virtue.

But in Maggie's case, it was a strength he yearned to solve.

He knew better than anyone else that looks could be deceptive. Women camouflaged what they considered physical weaknesses. They wore padded bras and high-heeled shoes. Men sucked in their beer guts and toned down their four-lettered vocabularies. Each gender had mastered the art of deception when it came to the rituals associated with the opposite sex until they were legally wed. Then the trappings were stripped, and the real person emerged.

But he couldn't forget the warm woman he'd held in his arms the night before. Maggie's fears had been real. She couldn't hide the frightened girl inside, and he hadn't been able to hide his desire to comfort her and make the world right again.

Her tears hadn't been a statement of weakness. On the contrary, Griff didn't think he knew a stronger woman than Maggie. He envisioned all the storms she'd ridden out alone. She'd never burdened BJ with the trauma of her scars. Neither had she sought professional guidance or a friend's presence.

The stiffness of her limbs told him how hard she worked to be strong.

He understood that kind of strength.

After his mother left, he never walked into a house without bracing himself for disappointment and ultimate loss. He'd learned to live for himself because it was safer.

The same held true for Maggie. She'd learned to rely only on herself.

Griff's fingers wrapped into a fist. Just thinking about all the times Maggie had had to weather her fears alone made him angry and want to protect her. Her aloneness bothered him a lot more than his ever had. He wanted to be her anchor and support.

You're in danger of becoming a besotted fool, Murdock. She doesn't need you or anyone else. It's better for her to be strong on her own. Anything else would encourage a false dependency.

His scolding didn't hold up against the picture of Maggie in his head. He wanted to sink into her arms and find the pleasure that he'd been denying himself.

Griff eyed his tight fists. For the life of him, he couldn't relax. If he did, neither that closed door nor his wounds would be able keep him away from the woman on the other side.

By late afternoon the next day, Maggie thought she'd go mad.

She and Griff reexamined each of the file folders again. It should have been a routine matter, something that would keep their minds active and channeled toward bringing the investigation to an end.

On the surface, they followed procedure. But even in the light of day, there was nothing routine about their actions.

She couldn't quite put a name on what made this discussion between two police officers different than any other. If anyone else walked into the room, he'd believe they were being totally professional.

But she and Griff were too careful not to touch each other when they passed the files between one another. Their conversation was stilted and to the point.

From the corner of her eye, she observed the tight grip Griff had on his jaw. She, on the other hand, had to concentrate hard to keep her hands from shaking whenever she accidentally brushed against him.

How much longer could they go on like this?

A whimpering sound caught Maggie's attention the next afternoon as she perused another of her father's case files. She'd been using all her energy to ignore the strained atmosphere infiltrating the four cedar walls.

The first time she'd heard the unfamiliar noise, she'd wondered if the wind was picking up.

Then she heard it again. She cocked her head and met Griff's dark gaze.

"Did you hear that?" she asked, rising to her feet.

"Maggie—"

She tuned out the warning note in his voice and

strode across the room. "It sounds like a wounded animal."

From behind her, she heard the chair Griff had been resting his leg on, crash to the floor. "Dammit, Maggie."

Before he could stop her, she slipped the lock and peered outside. She immediately spotted the sad-faced culprit quivering on the edge of the stoop. It was a small cream-colored dog.

She released the latch and swung wide the door.

"Ooh, you poor thing." She let him sniff her hand before scooping up the bedraggled animal and cuddling him to her breast. Checking the landscape, she noted that nothing else moved. "Where is your mama?"

The dog licked her hand as Griff came up behind her. "That was a fool thing to do."

"This little guy isn't going to hurt me."

"How did you know he wasn't a two-legged con man and carried a gun?"

"You don't think I can tell the difference between a man or an animal? Animals are much more trustworthy."

"Am I supposed to say 'ouch'?"

Maggie brushed by Griff as she closed the door, still carrying the lost dog. She didn't want to admit the puppy's cries overcame her good sense.

She sighed. "I wonder where he came from."

"Does he have a collar?"

"No. Maybe we should contact the police."

"They'll advise us to take him to the humane society." Griff surprised Maggie by reaching over and scratching behind the animal's ears.

"Someone could be looking for him."

"Not if he's been abandoned by one of the summer residents. According to several cops in the area, tourists are notorious for adopting pets and then dumping them after the season has ended."

Maggie's heart squeezed at the thought. "He looks so sad. I couldn't bear it if we took him to the pound and they decided to put him down."

Griff limped to the kitchen cupboard and pulled out a plastic bowl and filled it with water.

The puppy squirmed at the sight of the water dish Griff placed on the floor. Maggie released the animal and watched him dash to the bowl. "He's pretty thirsty. It won't hurt to wait awhile. If someone shows up, we can hand him over."

The sound of the dog's slurps filled the room.

"What are you going to call him?" Griff asked.

Maggie took a moment to consider him. One possibility leapt at her as she noticed the dissipation of the tension that had riddled the cabin earlier. "Let's call him Lucky. I think he's going to bring us good luck."

Griff shrugged. "It's as good a name as any."

The rest of the afternoon passed quickly. Maggie found scraps of food for Lucky, while Griff scrounged through a closet and found a box to make a bed for their new resident. Maggie pulled an old towel from a rag box under the bathroom sink to use for bedding.

Once their hungry guest had eaten, he settled down for a nap.

Maggie made an attempt at cutting a doll's skirt from some of the fabric she'd brought with her. However, she became easily distracted by the tug-of-war going on a few feet from her as Lucky and Griff battled each other for supremacy. Griff didn't seem bothered by the cast any longer. He'd maneuvered himself to the floor for greater accessibility to wrestle with his worthy opponent.

"You think you're tough, don't you, big guy?" Griff playfully taunted his feisty opponent.

Lucky kept his teeth clenched on the end of the old towel and gave a defiant toss of his head.

Maggie's lips curled into a smile.

Her dad had never liked animals. There were several occasions when she'd tried to sneak a cat or hamster into the house. No reason was ever good enough to convince BJ that Maggie should have a pet.

"You like animals," she said in the midst of their exuberant play. "Did you ever have a pet?"

Griff shook the cloth. "A couple of foster homes had dogs. But I was never allowed to get one of my own." Then he released his end and let the dog win the skirmish.

The puppy pranced around the room victoriously. Just as quickly, he dropped his trophy and returned to Griff's side, where he snuggled contentedly. Griff reached over and retrieved a glass of water with one hand, while he used his other to stroke his furry friend.

Maggie hadn't been prepared for Griff's gentleness with the canine. Maybe she was hoping he'd be gruff or ignore the puppy's antics, so he would be easier to hold at a distance.

"You'll make a great father some day." The words were out of her mouth before she had a chance to second-guess her thoughts.

The glass slid from Griff's fingers and crashed to the floor. The puppy yelped, startled by the sudden noise. But it was the sharp pain piercing Griff's face that caught Maggie's attention.

She sprang to her feet. "Your hand is bleeding."

She grabbed a paper towel from the kitchen spindle and ran cold water to moisten it.

"It's just a small cut," Griff said.

She squatted next to him and grabbed his hand. "A small cut can lead to a large infection."

He didn't pull away as she wrapped his injured limb and applied pressure to stop the blood flow.

She instantly became aware of how warm his skin was. Startled, her gaze lifted and locked with his. She saw the sudden need in his face and tried to swallow.

Dragging her gaze from his, she glanced at the wounded finger again. "I think the bleeding stopped."

"Yes."

Trying to look anyplace but at him, she picked up the pieces of broken glass and rose to her feet. After she deposited the shards into the trash, she returned to her chair by the couch. Even the puppy's presence couldn't cut through the tension.

"Thank you," Griff said.

She wasn't sure how to apologize. "I didn't mean to make you uncomfortable when I said you'd make a good father."

Griff's expression became remote. "I know."

"Didn't you want to have children with your wife?"

At first, she didn't think he was going to answer her. The only sounds in the cabin were Lucky's snuffling the few drops of water left on the floor.

Finally Griff spoke. "I always wanted a family more than anything in the world. When I married Sonja, I thought I had it all. A wife. A small apartment with the hopes of something bigger someday. A good job. Then she left me. And suddenly the dream was gone. It wasn't until the autopsy report came back that I discovered she was pregnant."

Maggie felt as if a giant fist slammed into her heart. "How could she do that?"

He didn't seem to hear her. "It was ironic. I didn't cry for Sonja. She'd killed whatever love we had when she'd left with another man. But I sobbed over the baby. He was a little boy. I don't know if he was mine or her lover's. It never mattered. The only thing that counted was that the child had died."

Maggie couldn't stand it. She found herself at Griff's side. Without worrying about the possible ramifications, she wrapped her arms around his shoulders and held him tight. His head rested against her breast.

There was no way to erase the hurt and anguish he'd gone through. Internal pain didn't magically disappear.

"I'm so sorry," she whispered, hoping he'd at least understand that he wasn't alone.

Moisture ran down her cheeks. At least she thought the tears belonged to her. Griff's tears would be silent, rooted deep within him.

How could he ever trust a woman again?

First his mother and then his wife. No wonder he empathized with an abandoned puppy. They'd both been the victims of people who had turned their backs on them and broken the fragile bonds of trust. Maggie found herself shaking her head in disbelief. How could people be so cruel and thoughtless?

Griff heard Maggie's heart thundering in his ear. For years he'd barricaded his emotions with a resilient mental armor, never willing to risk his heart to another woman. He'd chosen the safe road. The women he'd dated weren't interested in settling down. They favored men who were free and easy.

Everything he'd ever learned stood at the brink of toppling. He should be pulling free of Maggie's gentle hold and retreating to his icy fortress. He didn't want this type of intimacy.

His internal arguments fell on deaf ears. Maggie's arms were a haven he'd actively boycotted ever since he was a little boy. For the life of him, he couldn't move. Didn't want to.

If he moved, he'd hurt her feelings. Or so he tried to tell himself.

Why did he want to stay here forever, locked in Maggie's arms and nestled into her feminine warmth? He should be hornier than hell.

A growing heat in the lower part of his body told him that he was indeed turned on. And if this were any other woman, he wouldn't resist the urge to pull her into his arms.

But it wasn't sex that was making him hot and bothered. He wanted more, and that's what kept him from moving. He wanted to make love to Maggie, a desire that wasn't physical as much as emotional.

You're opening the door to certain heartache, a distant voice in the back of his head warned. He had to struggle to remember the pain of rejection and abandonment.

But this was Maggie—the woman who collected old-faced dolls and couldn't turn her back on a little lost dog.

Scenes over the past week paraded through his head. The bride walking down the aisle. Her steadfast hold on his hand when they'd ridden to the hospital. The taste of her lips in the ER.

A wave of sharp need rose within him. How could agony be so sweet and desperate at the same time?

Their marriage vows were as phony as a TV soap opera.

Maggie owed him nothing, and yet she'd stayed. And in staying, she'd put down roots.

He only had to look around the cabin and see the homey touches she'd already added. A picture of Maggie with BJ sat on the nightstand next to her bed. A well-washed afghan rested at the foot of the bed. A ratty stuffed animal slumped against her suitcase.

Did she ever discard anything?

Was this how she'd survived her lonely childhood?

He'd learned to live without.

Maggie had learned to make the most of what she had.

An old dream niggled at his subconscious. When Sonja had left, he'd resolutely, with no regrets, banished any desire to have a wife, two point four kids and a house with a white picket fence.

With his head pillowed into Maggie's softness, he had this overwhelming desire to cement the vows they'd exchanged in a way that would bind them forever.

You're going soft, Murdock. She's catching you on your blind side.

The crazy thing was, he didn't feel weak or vulnerable in Maggie's arms. Strength battled peace for supremacy. Hell, he really was crazy.

Fate had preordained a life of solitariness for him. He had put every bit of his energy into his job. That had always been enough for him.

A whine jarred him.

"What's the matter, sweetie?" Maggie asked the dog, who'd just wakened from his nap.

Maggie gently nudged Griff, and he forced himself to move so she could lift the small animal.

As Maggie straightened, Griff saw the flush of color adorning her cheeks and realized he wasn't the only one who was affected by their closeness.

"I should take him outside. He probably needs to run around a bit," she said before rising to her feet.

Griff knew he should be grateful for the canine's

presence. If the dog hadn't intervened, who knows what could have happened?

You'd have made love with her. That's what would have happened. Not even a cast or stitches would have stopped him.

Instead of the dashing of cold reality such a thought should have triggered, Griff found himself resenting the intrusion even more.

Maybe there was only one way to get rid of this foolish need. A quick bounce on the sheets would douse the burning lust and eliminate the sizzling tension between them.

How much longer before he bit the bullet and begged Maggie to put out the fire inside him?

He heard the outside door close behind Maggie. The silence became unbearable.

Left alone amidst her treasures and lingering scent, Griff noticed her absence even more.

You're in big trouble, Murdock. Big trouble.

Chapter 12

Because of Dwight Conrad's tracking their whereabouts, Wylie didn't return to the cabin for fear of someone following him.

The next week stretched on as Maggie unapologetically used Lucky's presence to enforce a dividing line between Griff and her.

Whenever the weather cooperated, she took the dog outdoors and played with him. The greatest danger to her sanity had become the increasing sexual awareness between Griff and her. She had trouble worrying about the unidentified shooter who was behind their forced retreat from Pendleton.

After Griff threatened to remove his cast himself, Wylie arranged for them to drive to the Michigan Upper Peninsula to see a local doctor.

It had been less than twenty-four hours since a

shorter cast had been put on, allowing Griff greater mobility.

And the atmosphere between them had become unbearable.

Maggie spent most of the morning outside, throwing sticks for Lucky to retrieve.

Griff had stayed inside, taking another stab at the police files.

It was the middle of the afternoon when he walked down to the dock.

An army of gooseflesh lined Maggie's arms as soon as Griff stepped outside.

Instantly she sensed a change. A new determination radiated from him. And she knew it had nothing to do with the case.

Grasping for composure, she kept her face trained away from him so he wouldn't see how raw and exposed she had become.

She'd been mentally kicking herself for her foolishness in attempting to comfort Griff. Nothing had been the same between them since then.

How could she have been so stupid as to take him into her arms? Griff Murdock wasn't a small child who needed a hug.

He was a strong man who could take care of himself.

The puppy took a flying leap into a pile of newly dropped leaves. Then he scampered back to Maggie. She reached down and rubbed his ears, earning a grateful lick in return.

As soon as she finished, the dog trotted over to Griff and collapsed at his feet.

Griff leaned down and patted the dog's head. The dog responded by flipping onto his back and letting Griff scratch his outstretched belly. "You're quite the little beggar, aren't you?" Griff asked.

A smile tugged at Maggie's mouth. "He's not afraid to ask for what he wants."

Griff's gaze zeroed in on hers. He didn't disguise the hunger radiating within him. "Maybe that makes him smarter than us."

"He's too young to know what's good for him."

"That's one theory. Or he could realize that life's too short, and each of us has to take advantage of the few opportunities that present themselves."

"Since when did you start speaking in clichés?"

"When did you start running?"

Desperation surged through her. "This isn't a good idea, Griff. We both should be running."

Griff shook his head. "That's what we've been doing and it hasn't worked. Has it?"

"This situation is unnatural."

"Wanting to make love is completely natural."

She almost gasped aloud as he laid his desire out in the open.

He hadn't moved a step, yet Maggie felt surrounded by him. She struggled to stay in control. "This Indian summer is undermining our good sense."

"The weather has nothing to do with the dreams I've been having."

"Nightmares?" She made a stab at being glib.

"No. More like fantasies woven with unfilled desires."

The glimmer of amusement appearing on Griff's

face should have lightened the atmosphere between them.

It did the opposite.

He was sexier, more approachable—dangerously so.

Maggie tried to contain the yearning to trace the creases on his face. He wasn't being fair. She couldn't think when he alluded to an ecstasy that would never last.

Or could it?

Griff's gaze burned into hers. "Have you ever wanted something so much that you were willing to risk your soul to have it?"

Her mouth dried at the expression on his face. "We wouldn't be here if it weren't for Dad."

Griff seemed to give her statement some thought. He looked down at the puppy curled at his feet before raising his gaze to hers again. Maggie saw the renewed determination in his expression. "You can't continue to throw BJ between us."

She should turn and walk away. That would be the smart thing to do. Her feet refused to move. "You're more of a risk than I'm sure I can handle."

"Maybe you think I'm just like Conrad and every other weak pervert."

He'd given her the perfect excuse to escape. She could hide behind the fears that had held her captive for too long.

Few men had ever earned her trust or respect. Why should she believe Griff was any different?

Because he was, the voice in the back of her head said.

But her personal code of ethics wouldn't let her evade the truth. In all the years she'd known him, Griff had never been anything but honest. He'd saved her from herself when she'd been caught shoplifting. If she'd continued her wild life of petty crime, she wouldn't have been able to look herself in the face as an adult. Griff could have ignored her and let her take the consequences.

Perhaps he'd wanted to save his partner from the repercussions of her actions. His reasoning didn't matter to her at this point. Griff had always been straight with her.

And that made him more lethal to her than any other man alive.

It also made him the most attractive.

"You're not anything like Dwight Conrad," she said.

"No."

"You're not like my father, either."

His gaze narrowed. "Don't paint any halos on me, Maggie. I'm still just a man."

"Is that a warning?"

"Do you need one?

"I'm not sure," she said. "What about you?"

"I've never been more scared in my entire life. The hunger I have burning for you inside me is bringing me to my knees. But I'm also tired of being semi-aroused from halfway across the room. If you don't want this, Maggie, then say so."

She shook her head. "That's the trouble. I do want it. I just can't see where it's going to lead. Where it will end."

He offered a half smile. "And after you find the answer to that, you can solve world hunger."

She looked away. "You don't want to get involved."

"So I keep telling myself. But my body refuses to listen."

"What are we going to do?"

He held out his hand to her.

The decision rested on her shoulders. The few feet of ground that separated them seemed filled with potholes.

The number of sexual encounters she'd had could be counted on one hand. But it wasn't a lack of experience that made her hesitate.

She'd always been able to hold back a part of herself when she'd been with a man. That had protected her from whatever disappointments she'd faced.

Would she be able to raise that same resistance against Griff?

That's what worried her.

"Maggie, come to me."

It was the need in his gray eyes that seduced her. She couldn't turn away from him, even if she'd wanted to. And the truth was, she didn't want to.

The moment her fingers touched his, time became nonexistent.

He didn't release her hand as he scooped the dog into his other arm and limped the few steps to the cabin.

Once inside, Lucky nestled into his homemade bed. Griff closed the bedroom door behind them and reached for her. Maggie thought she heard her own muffled groan as his mouth descended to hers.

The touch of his lips made her body sag into his. This wasn't like the public kiss in the ER. Griff took his time to thoroughly taste her, while she did her own sampling.

She hadn't realized her nerves could sing to the beat of her pulse rate. Every part of her body clamored with need.

She wanted to feel the heat of his skin against hers.

As soon as the thought came, she realized her hands were already yanking at the buttons on his shirt. Griff's were equally as busy, tugging at the lower edge of her short-sleeved sweater and lifting it over her head.

He tossed it aside and unclasped her bra, dragging it from her body and causing her nipples to harden.

"Ah, Maggie, you are incredibly beautiful. Do you have any idea how long I've dreamed of this?"

"How long?" She liked hearing the sound of his voice at the same time his hands caressed her bare skin.

"Since the day you showed up for work at the department."

Her fingers halted in their quest to unzip his pants. She remembered that day all too well. "You looked furious. I thought you wanted to lock me in a cell and throw away the key."

"I did." His slow, crooked grin made her heart pick up speed as the back of her knees bumped against the mattress. "But I wanted to be in that cell with you."

"Why didn't you tell me? Why were you so cold?"

He gently pushed her down on the bed and removed the rest of her clothes. "You were my partner's daughter and you hated my guts. I figured it was safer for both of us if I kept my distance. Neither of us was ready for this."

As he shucked off his jeans, she noticed his bandaged thigh. "Maybe we shouldn't do this. What about your injuries and—"

"I don't need a nurse. I need you." His words were accompanied by the shedding of his boxers.

Maggie forgot to breathe. He was beyond magnificent. His desire for her produced a rush of feminine power.

Why had she waited so long to make love to Griff? The ache inside of her was overwhelming.

"Griff." His name came out as a husky moan.

"What do you want, Maggie?"

"You."

He lowered himself onto the bed next to her and brought his lips down on hers. She wrapped her arms around his shoulders and reveled in the width of him.

This kiss was every bit as mind-boggling as the first one. It was both hot and sweet, accentuated by his hand stroking the curve of her hip.

She was equally as brazen with her caresses. He had an exceptional body, hard and toned, the kind that any artist would savor. Despite the growing ache in the midsection of her body, she took her time exploring each curve and indentation, loving the sexy growl she earned each time her palm found a new plateau.

He tasted male and sexy.

As she solved each new mystery, Griff performed his own investigation. His uninjured hand cupped the weight of her breast before his mouth caught the rigid nipple between his teeth and tugged.

Sharp desire shot through the core of her body.

"Griff," she moaned, hungering for the weight of his body upon hers.

He lifted his head. "You're so sensitive to my touch."

She reached out to grab his hand and halt his torment of her breast.

She tried to twist away, but he held her tight and lowered his fingers between her legs. The instant he touched her, she thought she'd explode.

"Let me touch you," she begged.

"If you do, I'll come apart."

Tension heightened in her body. He had total control of every nerve ending, and she instinctively tried to resist him by clamping her legs shut.

He stopped but didn't remove his hand. His gaze culled her secrets. "Do you want me, Maggie?"

"Yes." She could barely hear her own voice. She was beyond want.

"Then open your legs for me. Take me inside."

She didn't have to think twice as he released her hands and lifted over her. She reached down and guided him into her.

Her gaze connected with his as he drove deep inside her. He wasn't bothering to hide the depth of his need. He made her feel exquisite and cherished as his hands stroked her overly sensitive skin.

She'd never felt so much a part of anyone in her life. It was as if his body had become part of hers, and she didn't want it to end.

She clasped her hands around his shoulders and gloried in the heat and mastery of his possession. For each thrust, she met his.

The friction between them built. She thought she'd go crazy with the intense pleasure.

Her hips created their own primitive rhythm and Griff framed her face with his hands. "Slow down, Maggie, or we'll both go up in flames."

"I can't."

Before he could argue, she raked her hands down his back and rotated her pelvis in such a manner that ignited more friction between them.

"Maggie—"

His attempt to corral her movements came too late. A climax ripped through her at the same time Griff's shout muffled into her hair.

For a long moment afterward, neither of them could move. Griff finally pulled himself from her and rolled to his side.

"You're a dangerous woman."

"Why?"

"Because I wanted this to be special for you."

"What about for you?"

"It was perfect."

"Really?" Unable to resist, she used her index finger to trace his whiskered jaw. "On a scale of one to ten, I'd say that it was a six."

"You're awfully brazen for a naked woman."

"I can run faster than you."

Her retort made his eyes narrow. Then he leaned back and laughed.

Maggie leaned deeper into the covers and watched him collapse on the bed next to her, his chuckles ringing in her ear.

She'd never seen this side of Griff. There was no sign of the usual coolness he exhibited in the past to hold others at a distance.

It occurred to her how vulnerable she was at this moment. The true peril spun from the feelings she was beginning to have for the man at her side. She didn't want to just make love to him again; she wanted to be with him tomorrow and the next day.

Griff didn't want that kind of commitment.

Would he think she expected it?

Suddenly she felt very conscious of her nakedness. She quietly turned on her side and slipped to her feet.

"Where are you going?" Griff asked.

She reached for her shirt and pulled it over her head, feeling strangely exposed. "I thought I heard Lucky. He probably has to go outside."

"I don't hear anything."

Not bothering to answer, she swung open the door and hurried into the other room. Lucky raised his sleepy eyes and wagged his tail at the sight of her. He didn't seem eager to move from his bed. Nevertheless, she lifted him into her arms and carried him back into the bedroom.

Keeping her eyes away from Griff's naked body, she said, "I think he was missing us."

''You almost have him convinced.'' Griff's tone didn't mask his cynicism.

She knew the color was rising in her cheeks, but she refused to make any apologies. Lucky squirmed in her arms, so she set him on the bed.

Griff covered himself with a bedsheet as Lucky curled up next to his side. He saw Maggie grab up the rest of her clothes and dart into the bathroom. So much for his fabulous lovemaking skills. She couldn't wait to escape the bed.

Lucky snuggled closer to him. At least the dog liked him.

A few minutes later Maggie emerged from the bathroom.

''You didn't have to get dressed on my account,'' he said.

Her head jerked in a quick nod. ''I thought it was safer if one of us was clothed.''

He tried to search for hidden truths but couldn't scale the wall she'd resurrected between them. ''What happened, Maggie?''

She turned her head away from him so he couldn't decipher the thoughts whirling through her head. After a pregnant silence, she said, ''I've never been very good at pillow talk. I thought I'd just save us both from the awkwardness.''

He didn't buy her explanation. ''One of us must have been underwhelmed.''

Some of the rigidity left her body. ''You know better than that. Making love with you was like a glimpse of heaven.''

"But…?"

"Where do we go from here?"

"Does that question have to be asked now? We're not going anywhere."

"Then when?" she asked, with stark simplicity and no anger.

Griff wanted to ignore the truth in her words. "It's just sex."

She flinched at his brutal answer. "If that's all it was, then we should be able to walk away. Nothing lost. Nothing gained."

He wanted to argue but didn't know what to say. They should be able to walk away. Only he didn't want to.

Maggie plucked the dog from the bed. "I'll take Lucky into the other room before he considers the furniture in here a chew toy, too."

Griff heard rather than saw the door shut behind her as she left the room.

Damn!

It wasn't just sex. She knew it. He knew it.

The strong emotions swirling through him had nothing to do with their physical joining.

Maggie had pushed him away. Why did that hurt? *You pushed her away, too.* Neither of them wanted forever.

He'd set a course for his future that was formulated on being unattached with a whole heart. He didn't want any long-term emotional entanglements that would ultimately lead to heartache.

Why was he suddenly less concerned about the

risks of making a commitment than he was worried about a future without Maggie?

They'd made love. Exquisite love.

He still wanted her.

For how long? Until she left for good?

She'd been right to walk away now.

Now he had to find a way to live with that.

Chapter 13

Griff couldn't help but wish for a little thunder later that night so Maggie would need his comforting arms around her. Unfortunately, there wasn't a cloud in sight.

The sofa bed had become distinctly uncomfortable. And lonely.

Maggie had become an addiction.

When sleep didn't arrive by two o'clock, he took matters into his own hands. He walked quietly into the bedroom and lay across the top of the bed next to her.

Maggie tensed slightly as his arms came around her and pulled her against his body. "Relax," he murmured into her ear. "Nothing is going to happen. We're just going to sleep."

"Don't you want to get under the covers?" she murmured sleepily.

"No."

After a moment he heard her even breathing.

Getting inside the bedding and feeling her skin against his would undermine what little control he had left.

For now, he'd take comfort in holding her.

Griff didn't wake up the next morning until Maggie left the bedroom. A few minutes later he heard her giving a lecture to Lucky.

"No chewing on the furniture." She waved a stern finger at the guilty-looking puppy, not raising a hand but making her displeasure known in a firm caring voice.

Through the open doorway, Griff saw Lucky slink back into the bedroom with a crestfallen expression. Griff understood the feeling well.

Lucky came alongside the bed.

"Got yourself into a spot of trouble, did you, fella?" Griff reached over and drew the dog up next to him. Lucky wagged his tail and huddled close as his mistress's footsteps came closer.

"Come back here," Maggie called softly, peering into the room. She walked through the doorway and came to an abrupt stop when she realized Griff was awake. "Drat. I didn't mean to wake you."

Griff propped his hands behind his head. "What time is it?"

"Nine o'clock." Then she scowled at Lucky. "We're going to have to watch him. He's developed a taste for hardwood furniture."

"He's a puppy. Puppies like to chew."

"I'm sure that will appease Wylie when he discovers doggy bites at every corner of his sofa."

Griff couldn't hide his flinch as he swung his feet to the floor.

"Is your leg still bothering you?" she said. "You should have left the cast on."

"It'll heal faster if it has room to breathe."

"What did the doctor say?"

"It's my leg."

She shook her head. "Maybe you should stay in bed."

"Do you want to join me?"

She turned away from his probing gaze. "I'm going to take Lucky outside."

Before he could argue, she opened the door and Lucky dashed outside.

Griff leaned back against the bed and brushed his fingers through his hair.

It was no wonder she'd fled. He was stoking the simmering fires that threatened to burn out of control whenever they were together.

He lowered his arms and inhaled the scent of Maggie on the pillow. If only he could have Maggie there, too.

When he woke an hour later, he showered and was fixing himself a bowl of cereal when a disheveled Maggie stepped into the cabin with a very dirty dog.

"Which one of you won the war?" Griff asked, fighting back a grin at the sight of them.

"Lucky thought he'd take a swim in the puddle by the shed. He had such a good time, he decided to share it with me.'' She caught sight of herself in the mirror by the coat hooks and groaned. ''Guess I won't have to worry about my wardrobe for the local beauty pageant.''

Griff thought she looked better than any of the model-thin contestants. Maggie was all woman, with curves that fit perfectly against his body.

Don't go there, Murdock. Or you'll both end up back in bed.

He eyed the dog, who was sniffing the floor near the kitchen counter. The puppy didn't seem the least bit repentant. He wagged his tail, oblivious to the brown muck drenching his fur. ''He seems to have had a good time.''

''Do you want to clean him up?'' she asked darkly.

Griff was starting to feel a lot better than he had a short time ago. Bantering with Maggie restored his spirits, even if it didn't answer any life-changing questions. ''The doctor said I should keep off this leg whenever possible.''

''Ah. So now you're the victim.'' Maggie turned her back on him and refocused on Lucky. ''Come on, you need a bath.''

Griff finished his breakfast while Maggie turned on the bathroom faucet.

A few minutes later he heard the click of nails against the wood floor as Lucky came tearing around the corner.

''Lucky, get back here,'' Maggie ordered.

She came out of the bathroom and found the dog cowering behind Griff.

''Need some help?''

"I thought you were playing the victim."

"I took my vitamins."

Maggie felt rumpled and out-of-sorts next to the man whom she couldn't erase from her senses no matter what she did.

Why had he come into bed with her last night?

Why had she let him?

He fueled a need inside her that she hadn't sought. Now she wasn't sure how she was going to live the rest of her life without him.

She tried to keep her feelings from showing on her face. "The bath is ready, but he seems to have an aversion to clean water."

The small dog proved to be a handful, and it took both of them to maneuver him into the tub. Even then, he did everything in his power to squirm from the white porcelain cell and escape the soapy torment.

Griff sat on the edge of the stool while Maggie squatted along the side. In the tiny confines of the bathroom, there was no way to avoid touching each other.

She poured soap into her hands while Griff constrained the dog.

The puppy's sad eyes tugged at her heartstrings. "It's okay, sweetie. You're going to feel much better when you're all nice and clean," she crooned, lathering the wet fur.

Lucky whined.

"You'll be the best-looking dog in this neck of the woods."

"You sound like a proud mother," Griff drawled.

"Better watch out or you'll end up with a dog on your hands."

Her fingers accidentally brushed against his as she massaged the suds. She tried not to show any reaction, even though she was acutely aware of how close he was. "He should have a place where he can run, dig and play."

"And if he doesn't?"

Lucky had quit struggling and was looking at her with his big wistful eyes. She dabbed the foam from his nose. "Then I'll keep looking until he has the perfect home."

"You could take him to the pound."

"No, I couldn't."

Her green eyes flashed with defiance as her chin rose. Griff had to force himself not to pull her into his arms and take her right here in the bathroom.

Why this woman?

Maggie was exactly the kind of complication he didn't need. He'd vowed never to risk that kind of rejection again. Hadn't he learned anything?

Yet each time Maggie's hands touched his, he had trouble remembering anything other than the look and feel of Maggie. His intense hunger for her was growing. He'd thought that making love to her would satiate the lust.

The very opposite had happened.

He wanted her more.

Last night the fantasies he'd woven in his youth had returned in electrifying color. Only this time he could see the face of the woman he'd wanted to build a life with. The face belonged to Maggie.

"Griff?" Her voice jarred him. "Are you okay?"

He realized she'd rinsed all the foam from the dog, who was starting to shiver. "We need to dry him off."

Griff helped her lift the dog. Then he stood up and stepped aside so she had room to gently towel dry the dog.

Her damp T-shirt molded her nipples.

With sheer force, he dragged his gaze away, noticing how Lucky, who was now free of the dreaded tub, had nestled against her with trust and adoration.

A lump formed in his throat. "You're going to be a great mother someday."

She stopped rubbing. "I don't know anything about being a mother."

"Yes, you do. It's not about knowledge. It's a matter of instinct."

"And what would I do about a father for my child?" She slowly lowered the towel and turned toward him. "A child needs a father. And I'm not sure I could trust another man to embrace that kind of responsibility."

"Not all men are like your father."

"Too many are. You know what they say—you pick what you know. I seem to hit the bull's-eye every time."

"You don't want to be a mother?"

"I refuse to selfishly deny a child a father." Releasing the dog, she stood up, her posture tall and defiant. "What about you? You were married once."

"It was a mistake."

"You loved her, didn't you?"

"I'm not sure I knew what love was. I wanted to

create a family album, so I found a woman who fit the picture in my head. When she figured it out, she walked out the door.''

''Did she walk or did you push her?''

''What does that mean?''

''Maybe you were so sure she'd leave, you made it impossible for her to stay.''

''That sounds like a woman's excuse.''

A long, measured silence was Maggie's answer.

''I'm sorry. That was a cheap shot,'' Griff said. In truth, Griff didn't want to believe her accusation. Had he ever really trusted Sonja? He'd rushed Sonja down the aisle before she had a chance to know him. Had that been so she wouldn't have time to think, to recognize the personal fears he'd been hiding?

''We're quite a pair, aren't we?'' Maggie said, not able to hide her regret.

''That should make us safe to each other.''

She hugged her arms across her body as if trying to still a shiver. ''I don't feel safe.''

Griff watched her as she tore her gaze from his and walked out of the room. With a little difficulty, he rose to his feet and followed her to the kitchen.

Maggie stood in front of the refrigerator, surveying the contents before putting a dish of leftovers on the floor for the hungry dog.

She was right. They weren't safe. Despite all arguments to the contrary, he yearned for the unattainable. He wanted Maggie, pure and simple. The infamous control that he'd mastered over the years bordered on the brink of disaster. But he wasn't sure that he wouldn't push her away, too.

"Is there an extra fishing pole in that shed?" he asked.

Relief loosened the stiffness of her posture. "There's one for each hand, if you'd like."

"One is about all I can handle."

He couldn't help but notice the striking metaphor could equally apply to his relationship to Maggie. She was the only woman any man could want or need.

Someday, there would be a man smart enough to recognize the riches Maggie had to offer and win the trust she was reluctant to give.

Maggie bent down to remove the dish from the floor. Her shirt shifted, revealing the ripe curve of her firm buttocks. She straightened and walked toward the door. Turning the knob, she looked back at him. "Coming?" she asked.

"Go on ahead, I'll be there in a minute."

Griff saw the questioning tilt to her head. But she didn't query him about his sudden reticence. He had to quench the storm brewing inside him.

Anger at the notion that another man could eventually win Maggie warred with the intense desire to make love to her until she agreed never to look at another man.

He had to get himself under control. But he wasn't sure that was possible anymore. Now that he'd made love to Maggie, he couldn't stand the idea of her with anyone else, and it was driving him crazy.

Chapter 14

Griff finally joined her at the dock twenty minutes later.

Maggie was relieved that he seemed determined to keep their conversation light as they took advantage of the good weather.

The gun holstered at Griff's side was the only hint of the true reason they were at the lake. He'd started carrying it with him, even when they walked down to the dock.

They didn't discuss the case or engage in a discussion about what lie between them. Maggie resolutely forced her convoluted feelings for Griff to the back of her mind.

While Griff cast his fishing line with his left arm, still needing to favor his right one, Maggie regaled him with some of Wylie's outrageous stories about the "big ones" that got away as they hooked smallmouth bass and threw them back in.

Against the lazy backdrop surrounding the picturesque lake, they covered every topic of conversation from the future of public education to her proposed business plans for the Victorian doll shop.

This must be what it's like to be a real married couple, Maggie thought. They were able to separate themselves from the simmering sexual tension and talk like normal people. There was an absurd yet comforting peacefulness to the scene.

For once, she chose to indulge in the fantasy that this was a real marriage. Make-believe was far safer than reality. If only she could forget about the passion they shared, or banish the realization that all of this would soon come to an end.

The sun was beginning to slide behind the trees when Griff reeled in his line and set down his fishing pole before he slapped a bug on his forearm. "The mosquitoes are starting to come out of hiding. You ready to go inside?"

Lucky, who had been dozing with one eye open under a tree, perked up and began to wag his tail.

The thought of returning to the cloistered confines of the cabin produced a hollow pit inside Maggie's stomach. She didn't look forward to the evening ahead. "We should contact Wylie and tell him we're not going to stay here much longer."

A tight line formed across Griff's mouth. "Running already?"

Irritation flashed through Maggie. "Stop trying to

equate me with your wife or mother. I'm not running away.''

His eyebrow hitched to a derisive angle before he turned away.

She watched him gather their fishing equipment and start toward the shed. Did he really believe she was looking for an excuse to leave him?

If only it were true.

In actuality, she wasn't sure how much longer she could live in the same house with him without falling head over heels in love with him. Self-preservation was her last line of defense.

Lucky followed close as Maggie hiked the narrow, tree-lined path back to the cabin. But as they entered the clearing surrounding the house, she stopped short at the sight of a thin manila envelope propped against the door.

She gazed around the small clearing. Everything appeared quiet and peaceful. She cautiously mounted the steps as Griff emerged from the woods behind her.

''Where did that come from?'' he asked.

Without touching it, she said, ''I suspect the local mail carrier delivered it.''

Griff picked it up. ''It's addressed to both of us at this location.''

He slit open the side. A single piece of paper fell into his hand.

Peekaboo, I found you!

''Is there anything else inside?'' Maggie asked.
''No.''

"We need to contact Wylie,"

"Do you have your car keys?"

"They're in the cabin."

Griff reached into his shirt and drew out his gun. The relaxed man had been replaced by the professional cop. "We'll check out the cabin, grab your keys and my phone before we head into town."

He opened the door. "Hold on to the dog," he said tersely.

Lucky seemed to understand their caution and stayed close to Maggie's side. It didn't take long to determine they were still alone, and whoever delivered the letter hadn't been inside the cabin.

Maggie retrieved her keys as Griff collected his cell phone. They stowed Lucky in the back seat of the station wagon after locking the cabin door.

"Do you think it's Conrad?" she asked.

"Only if he's more of a fool than I think he is. He has to know that we've notified the PD about his visit."

The cutting remoteness in Griff's response caused Maggie to give him a sideways glance. The approachable man who'd enjoyed a day of fishing had disappeared. His face had donned an all-too-familiar chiseled professionalism.

Probing his thoughts would yield little. She'd spent years trying to get her father to open up to her. Even after she joined the department, he'd resisted her overtures.

How foolish of her to forget what Griff was and always would be. A cop.

The gun attached to his side had more heart.

Clutching the steering wheel, she hoped he wouldn't realize how battered her emotions were.

Sometime over the past few weeks, she'd lowered her precious guard.

"Turn down this road," Griff directed abruptly.

She frowned. "This isn't the quickest route to town."

"I want to see if anyone is following us."

"The package was postmarked. The mailman delivered it."

"And it was addressed to the cabin. We don't know where our shooter is. He might be trying to draw us out."

Maggie took the road Griff indicated. The sun was beginning to set, producing an eye-squinting glare off the back window.

Griff glanced down at his cell phone. "Pull over. We're in digital range. I'll make the call from here."

Once they were parked, Maggie stared straight ahead as she listened to Griff give Wylie an update.

"No, we're not going to find a motel," Griff said tersely. "Let this guy come after us. It's time to draw him out of his hole."

Griff had clearly taken charge of the investigation, which was fine with Maggie. She wanted to put this fiasco and Griff behind her as soon as possible.

Thirty seconds later, Griff snapped shut the phone.

"Where to?" she asked.

"The cabin. We'll take turns sleeping tonight."

She slid him a mocking glance. "You sure you trust me to do that?"

"Is that a subtle jab that I'm bossy?"

"Not at all. I always enjoy being dictated to."

Griff didn't respond while she pulled the car back onto the highway.

After they entered the main road, Griff broke the silence. "Only one of us can be in charge."

"Right."

He sighed. "You want to flip for it?"

Suspicion made her cautious. "Would you let me take charge if I won?"

"Only if we used my two-headed coin, and I made the first call."

She shook her head. "That's what I thought."

"It's only fair, you know."

She glanced at Griff and saw the amusement on his face. "How's that?"

"I've let you have your way with me for the past few weeks."

"I must have missed something."

"You were the one in charge due to my injury."

She pursed her lips in disbelief. "Name one thing that you haven't controlled."

"I've never let a woman drive me," he said without emotion. "You're the first."

Her hands flexed against the steering wheel. "You didn't have a choice with your leg."

"I could have insisted Wylie get me a car with hand controls." He paused and let her assimilate his statement before adding, "I've always thought you were a good cop, Maggie."

Maggie didn't know if Griff was feeding her a line or not. "But...?"

"I don't think it ever made you happy."

She considered that for a moment. "You're saying that being a cop makes you happy?"

"No, but it's safe."

His cryptic answer left her momentarily speechless. Before she could respond, she spotted a light-colored pickup coming down a hill toward them.

At the sight of them, it slowed.

When they drew abreast, he pulled onto the shoulder of the road.

Griff glanced back. "He's turning around."

"Did you see his face?"

"No. He had it tucked into his collar."

She caught sight of the dusty pickup in her rearview mirror. He'd sped up and was closing in on their bumper. The exit to the cabin loomed a quarter of a mile ahead.

"Take the service road," Griff ordered.

She started to slow down, and then saw the vehicle charge her.

"Hang on," she shouted. "He's going to ram us."

She stabbed at the accelerator, making a last-ditch effort to outrun him.

But just then, a slow moving Buick coasted from the intersection in front of her and turned on to the highway.

Maggie jammed on her brakes to avoid hitting the car as the pickup hit them from behind.

The force caused Maggie's head to hit the side window.

Griff grabbed the wheel. Bracing for another bump, he pulled hard and headed toward the ditch. He heard rather than saw the truck roar past as he tromped down on the brake pedal with his good foot, bringing them to a sudden stop.

Griff took a deep breath. "Maggie—"

The old man, who had been driving in the Buick, tapped on the broken window. "Are you two all right?"

Griff noticed the dilation of Maggie's pupils and a jagged cut on her forehead. She was conscious, but just barely. "Don't move," he ordered.

Lucky whimpered in the back seat.

It took Griff a few seconds to force his car door open. His arm and leg were a bit sore from the sudden jarring, but he didn't notice any sharp pangs.

The older man tried to dislodge Maggie's but couldn't budge it.

Griff gently pulled Maggie toward him, lifting her in his arms.

"We need to get you to a hospital."

"No," Maggie said, her voice husky.

"Yes. You need to see a doctor."

"Do you always have to sound like a cop, Murdock?" she complained.

Even though he had to strain to hear her low voice, he was relieved to hear her banter. "Too bad that bump didn't knock out some of your sassiness, Bennington."

She winced as Griff set her into the back seat of the older modeled vehicle. He climbed in next to her and lowered her head against his shoulder.

The old man reclaimed his place behind the wheel, with Lucky riding shotgun.

"Thanks for stopping, Mr...?" Griff said.

"Beckwith. We live over that hill. I never saw you coming."

"Wasn't your fault. Did you get a look at the guy in the pickup?"

"The guy who hit you?" Mr. Beckwith shook his silver-haired head. "He tore past me faster than some of those young kids do on a Saturday night."

"Ever seen that vehicle before?"

"No. Of course, we get a lot of tourists around here over the summer and weekends. Could be a leftover."

Griff had to set aside his questions as arrived at the small, one-story hospital on the edge of town.

For now he was more concerned about Maggie's injuries than the whereabouts of the guy who'd run them off the road.

An hour and a half later, Griff sat next to Maggie's hospital bed after a brief update to Wylie.

Maggie now sported a bandage over her stitched cut and wore a shapeless hospital gown. The doctor had insisted she spend the night for observation due to her concussion. Griff came out with a few nasty bruises but no further damage to his recovering limbs.

"When is Wylie arriving?" she asked.

"He's already at the cabin and working with the local authorities to track down that pickup. I caught part of the license plate before he hit us."

She winced at the memory. "Where's Lucky?"

"Our new friend Mr. Beckwith took him home. They seemed to take to each other."

"He lives in the country, doesn't he?"

"Just a few miles outside the city limits."

She tried to nod her head, but the effort was too much.

"How's your head?" he asked.

"If I wasn't seeing double, I could do a two-step at the local dance hall."

"Once your head is healed and my leg is mobile, we'll make it a date."

Her heart pained. "You don't have to stay with me."

"Go to sleep, Maggie. I'm not going anywhere."

Even if she'd wanted to, Maggie couldn't stop her eyelids from closing. There was no question she felt safe and protected with Griff in the room.

But she couldn't help but wish it was more than a sense of duty that made him stay.

Chapter 15

Wylie showed up at the hospital the next morning as Maggie was finishing breakfast.

Griff looked disgustingly refreshed for having slept the night in a hospital chair. She, on the other hand, felt like she'd spent the night downing a keg at the local bar.

Her godfather deposited a kiss on her forehead. "Nice pair of black eyes you have, kitten."

She wrinkled her nose at him. "I want combat pay for this little assignment."

"Because of that itty-bitty bump on your head?"

"How bad is my car?"

"It's got a few dings, but you should be able to drive it."

Griff spoke up for the first time. "Did they find that driver yet?"

Wylie perched on the edge of the bed. "They found

the pickup parked in front of a country motel and arrested the owner first thing this morning.''

Griff leaned forward. ''Who is it?''

''He's not talking, but the description matches the guy BJ sent to jail for killing his stepson.''

''Joe Flint?''

''That's the guy. They need you to stop down at the police station and see if you can ID him. He had a gun. We'll run some tests and see if it matches the slugs we took from the church.''

Griff nodded. ''I'll do it as soon as we drop Maggie back at the cabin. The doctor is letting her check out, on the condition she stays in bed for the rest of the day.''

''I can stay in the car while you're in the station,'' Maggie said.

''It's either here or the cabin,'' Griff said.

Wylie chuckled. ''You two sound more married each day.''

Maggie glowered at them both.

An hour later, Griff and Wylie deposited Maggie at the cabin.

As Wylie checked the nearby area for any signs that Flint had been in the area, Griff made sure Maggie had everything she needed while they were gone.

She glared at him. ''I'll never get any sleep if you keep hovering over me.''

''There's a police officer stationed outside. Where's your weapon?''

She gestured toward the chair. ''Inside my purse.''

Griff picked it up and moved it next to the bed.

Maggie closed her eyes, praying he'd leave before she did something stupid. Having him fuss over her was almost more than she could stand. Her emotional reserves were at their lowest state. The tears building in the back of her eyes had nothing to do with her injury.

A few minutes later she heard Griff leave the small house, quietly shutting the door behind him.

Another moment or two passed. The muted slam of car doors preceded the hum of the engine.

Finally, she was truly alone. She could no longer hold the tears at bay. The emotional events over the past few weeks tumbled through her head.

Soon there would be no reason for her to ever see Griff Murdock again. They could annul the marriage and each go their separate ways.

Her stomach cramped at the thought, and she had to draw her legs up against her body to stifle the hurt.

The last person in the world she'd ever wanted to fall in love with was Griff. He was a cop. A man who had learned to divorce himself from any emotions and attachments. She'd known that before she ever agreed to participate in the wedding sting.

But that was before she had lived under the same roof for three weeks. She'd seen sides of him that she'd never believed existed: his playfulness with Lucky, his sense of humor, his comforting her during the thunderstorm and his vigilance at the hospital.

She couldn't forget his tenderness when he'd held her the night before.

A groan of despair tormented her.

What woman could resist a man who protected her?

It wasn't fair.

She had to remember that Griff had an overzealous sense of duty. He'd have done it for any person because he would have considered it part of his job. It didn't matter who she was.

Had that been the case when they made love?

Had she just been any face, any woman to him?

He'd spent a lifetime erecting his own iron bars against women. First his mother, then his wife.

What woman could leap the hurdles these two women had cemented into place?

He'd even lost his child.

How could he forgive such a loss?

Maggie hadn't been the one who betrayed him. How could he ever open himself to a second chance?

She didn't think she'd be able to.

Maggie touched her midsection. She'd never allowed herself to want a child. But now there was a steep aching want inside her.

She wanted Griff's child.

She might as well have wished for the moon.

Chapter 16

Griff fidgeted in the seat next to Wylie. They came up to a Y-intersection on the county road, and Griff found himself pressing the floor as if he had a brake.

"You okay?" the older man asked.

"I don't like riding."

Wylie chuckled. "How did you manage letting Maggie drive?"

"I got used to it."

He'd gotten used to her.

Griff didn't like the idea of leaving Maggie unprotected. Another officer didn't seem like enough protection.

He only trusted himself.

Was he starting to let paranoia take control of his senses?

They had a suspect in custody. Yet his gnawing uneasiness continued to build.

The blow to her head made her more vulnerable than being in the cabin with only one guard. He couldn't shake the feeling that he should be with her.

She hadn't wanted him to stay. She'd all but pushed him out of the cabin, obviously looking forward to severing any connection between them.

He gripped the armrest, bracing himself for the fresh onslaught of pain. The agony he experienced had nothing to do with Wylie driving the car or the residual effects from the gunshot wound in his leg.

What if he never saw Maggie again? She wasn't planning to stay in Pendleton. With BJ gone, there would be little reason for her to return.

Why should she want to? She wanted a new life that wouldn't involve a cop and the memories of her childhood.

The termination of their so-called marriage could be handled without either of them being present for the final decree.

Why does it bother you, Murdock?

The vows were part of the job.

Were they?

Then why did he want to yank the steering wheel from Wylie's hands and turn the car around?

Because you love her.

"We need to go back," Griff tersely broke the silence.

"What's the matter?" Wylie asked, but started to slow the car.

"I shouldn't have left her."

If Wylie thought he'd fallen off his rocker, he didn't say anything about it, not even a teasing remark.

Thirty seconds later, they were headed back toward the cabin.

Back to Maggie.

Exhaustion claimed Maggie's battered body. Despite her tired state, she couldn't erase the pictures in her head. She dreamed of making love to Griff again and again until he fell in love with her. She slid deeper into the fantasy, savoring the vivid illusion.

Just the memory of Griff's mouth touching hers brought a smile to her lips. He was firm and hard. She tried to tell him how much he meant to her. But something was stopping her.

She couldn't breathe.

A pillow blocked the air from reaching her lungs.

She brought her hands up to lift it and discovered another pair pressing the pillow against her face.

Someone was trying to suffocate her!

She twisted her body to escape her attacker. But the person on the other end held the advantage, using his body to smother her.

Dizziness swam through her head. Her lungs screamed for relief.

She raised her hips and tried to buck off her faceless assailant. For a brief moment, she caught him off-guard. A whiff of air brushed her face.

Before she could take advantage of his lapse, she was pushed back again. Her struggles became weaker.

She was dying.

She wished she'd told Griff she'd loved him. It was her only regret.

Just as consciousness faded, she suddenly found her head free.

"Maggie!"

Griff?

Blackness swam through her head as she dragged air into her aching lungs and tried to make sense of what was happening around her.

The lamp on the night-stand flew as Griff wrestled her attacker to the bed.

Wylie charged through the door with his gun posed in front of him.

"You okay?" Griff kept tight control of his captive as he lifted his head and tracked Maggie's ragged breathing.

"Yes," she rasped, pulling herself off the bed. As much as she hurt, she refused to lie on the bed a moment longer.

She moved to Griff's side and watched him tug the hood from his captive.

Maggie gasped.

Mrs. Harris. Griff's landlady.

"Why?" Maggie asked, although her voice was little more than a rasp.

"You fool!" the older woman spat at her. "You should be dead. As dead as my son."

Griff maneuvered his body to keep the woman from hitting Maggie. "Your son?"

"Frank Rankin."

Wylie shook his head, producing a pair of handcuffs that he handed to Griff. "Rankin died two years ago. He had nothing to do with Maggie."

"My Frank is dead because of *her* father."

"Rankin committed suicide," Griff countered. "BJ didn't kill your kid. He died by his own hand after the judge sentenced him to ten years in prison."

Mrs. Harris's eyes filled with venom. "Frank was too sensitive to survive in there. He was innocent. It was his word against the almighty BJ Bennington. Every time Frank came up for parole, the cop testified against him saying he was a sexual predator who had killed once and would kill again. Frank couldn't take it anymore so he killed himself."

"BJ is dead, too."

"But not his daughter." The woman tried to make a threatening move toward Maggie, but couldn't free herself from Griff's grasp. "Why shouldn't she have to suffer for all the pain I've had to endure?"

Maggie could almost feel sorry for the woman.

There was little sympathy in Griff's face, however.

"We've got Joe Flint in custody and he's admitted to the shooting outside the church as well as running the station wagon off the road," Wylie said. "How did you hook up with him?"

She tossed her head. "He shared the same cell block as my Frank. Joe hated the cop as much as I did. He figured no one would ever link us because my name was different."

"You didn't share the same surname with your son?" Griff commented.

She raised her chin. "'Harris' is my third husband's name."

"How long were you married to Rankin's father?"

"Too long."

"There's no record that you're Rankin's mother."

His question infuriated her. "My second husband didn't like kids, especially someone else's. Few men want the leavings of another man. I knew Franklin would have a better life with his real father. I was a good mother."

"Is that how you justified turning your back on your kid and walking away?" Griff asked, derisively.

"He understood. He knew I loved him."

"I'm sure that knowledge was a great comfort to him."

Any pity Maggie might have had for the bereft mother evaporated.

It amazed her that Mrs. Harris didn't seem to sense her personal danger.

Griff's tight-lipped expression revealed how much he was struggling to keep his temper under control as the older woman conveniently ignored any responsibility for her son's behavior and tried to transfer the blame to others.

Griff had to despise his former landlady and her flimsy excuses, but he didn't allow his personal feelings to show. Only Maggie seemed to see the effort it cost him.

Wylie stepped forward. "How did you get past the officer out front?"

The unrepentant woman sniffed. "Even the men in blue take potty breaks."

"Too bad your cleverness will be wasted in prison."

Mrs. Harris tried to sidestep Griff as Wylie handed him a pair of handcuffs. "I want to see a lawyer."

"I'll bet you do."

Griff relinquished his former landlady to Wylie as a local deputy entered the cabin.

After Mrs. Harris was tucked into one of the waiting police cars, Wylie returned to the house. "Do you two want to stay here or head back to Pendleton?"

Without looking in Griff's direction, Maggie said, "If my car is ready, I'm ready to leave."

Wylie's gaze flickered between them. "With that head injury, you shouldn't be driving, Maggie. I'll book Mrs. Harris and swing by to pick you up. That okay with you, Griff?"

Griff masked his feelings behind a stoic façade.

Maggie's hasty desire to leave scraped his emotions raw.

He shouldn't have been surprised. The job was over. She had no reason to stay.

They both wanted to reclaim the threads of their lives.

So why wasn't he ready to let go?

Chapter 17

Wylie's departure created a vacuum of silence between them as Griff and Maggie packed their belongings.

He'd tried to encourage Maggie to rest, but she'd refused to lie down on the bed again.

For the first fifteen minutes, they worked in separate rooms. Griff collated the files he'd spread across the coffee table. Maggie stuffed her clothes into the suitcase in the bedroom.

Griff took his time emptying the drawers and closets of the few items he'd brought with him.

He didn't realize Maggie had returned until he bumped into her as she came abreast of the sofa. The suddenness of their collision nearly knocked Maggie off her feet. Griff's hands automatically reached to steady her.

The firm swell of her curves undermined his resolutions.

"Maggie," was all he could say.

Her startled, green-eyed gaze met his. "I'm sorry."

"For what?"

She shook her head as if she didn't understand the question.

Her hesitation was all he needed.

He pulled her to him as she lifted her mouth. Her scent, womanly and soft, stoked the fires he'd worked so hard to bank. She wore her old jeans and the long-tailed shirt. He didn't think he'd ever seen a more enticing woman. Beneath the shapeless clothing, his hands framed the gentle curves of her hips. His manhood responded.

Suddenly they were pulling at each other's clothes.

Maggie's arms looped around Griff's neck as he picked her up and laid her on the bed. As he came down next to her, she reached up and stroked his face.

It was more than a starving man could stand. Griff found the curve of her neck and placed small kisses along the delicate arch of her jaw.

Maggie answered by threading her fingers through his hair and wrapping her legs around his torso.

"Your body should be put into protective custody," he groaned.

"Why?"

"It's too soft to be left unguarded."

He didn't want to think about what would happen after Wylie returned. Or the long, lonely months ahead. For now, this is where he wanted to be—in bed with the woman who'd staked a claim on his heart and his soul.

He'd learn to live with it later.

The packing forgotten, they explored each other's bodies. Intent on revealing each of her secrets, Griff rotated his body and lifted Maggie above him.

She slid onto him and for a moment neither of them moved. The pleasure in her face matched his own exhilaration.

She ran her fingers down the center of his chest and traced the ridge of his rib cage.

He sucked in a sharp breath. The intense pressure swirled from the center of him. Heaven could never be so sweet. So hot. He wanted to commit each facet of her lush form to memory.

Somehow this woman had gotten underneath his skin. He wanted her pleasure more than he wanted his own. He had always been able to keep a distance from other women. But he knew that whatever barriers he'd had were long gone with Maggie. He didn't even want to worry about tomorrow.

Maggie held nothing back, either. She moved slowly and made sure he was with her at every thrust of her pelvis.

"This can't be real," he breathed.

She stopped her movements. "I don't think it is."

"What is it then?"

Before he could catch his breath, she reached down and brushed a kiss across his brow. "Make-believe."

He answered by easing his hands through the thick hair at the nape of her neck. "Nothing ever felt so good."

"For me, either."

Her admission cut the little resistance Griff had left. He wrapped his arms around her and rolled her under him.

His thrusts deep inside her became more urgent. She shifted and took him deeper.

He was drowning and glad of it.

The explosion that ripped through him was like none he'd ever experienced as Maggie's body stiffened and followed him over the edge.

Griff collapsed on top of her and together they rode the rest of the storm.

He didn't know how long they lay in the tumble of sheets, their limbs entwined and their bodies still joined.

"Wylie will be coming soon," Maggie finally broke the silence.

"Yeah." He didn't want to move.

Her finger skimmed his whiskered cheek. "You need a shave."

"Are you volunteering to have another go at it?"

Her green gaze softened. "Hey, I didn't do too bad for my first time, did I?"

"You were perfect."

Hell, she was exquisite.

She suddenly lifted her head and propped her head to stare at him with sober eyes. "I wanted to hurt Mrs. Harris when she justified her actions for leaving her son."

"Why?"

She shook her head. "All I could think about was

your mother and wonder why she could have left you.''

Griff's mouth dried. ''Is that why you made love to me? For pity?''

A remote coolness shuddered her face. ''Is that what you believe?''

He didn't move for a minute, trying not to dwell on the sudden ache beating inside his chest. Why had she made love to him?

Not for love.

That was clear.

A cold fear descended over him. Why would he expect more? There were no commitments between them. What they had was a history of distrust and a phony marriage license.

Maggie pulled away. She found her clothes scattered across the floor but paused to look at him. ''I think we're both too scared to let go of the past.''

Then she slipped into the bathroom and closed the door behind her.

Was she right?

The past rose like a ghostly apparition.

Had Maggie made love to him to comfort him for his mother's actions nearly thirty years ago?

Would it be so bad if she had?

Griff's mouth twisted at the painful irony. He didn't feel comforted.

He remembered little of his mother's leaving. He'd made it his life mission to survive. And he'd done it.

But his mother's betrayal paled in the face of the future without Maggie.

Unwittingly, he'd laid himself open to her and

fallen in love. Now he was naked and his heart was bleeding.

Maggie leaned against the sink and struggled with ragged breaths.

What have you done, Maggie? How could you have placed yourself into such a vulnerable position?

She hadn't made love to Griff because she pitied him. He'd never believe the truth, and perhaps that was for the better. The only thing they could give each other was hurt. He saw her as the woman who'd abandoned her father.

And she'd never put herself at the disposal of living with another cop.

It was only a matter of time before he returned to his job. His injuries were healing nicely. Even with his short cast, he barely limped. Nothing had hindered his lovemaking. There was little to delay his return to the Pendleton Police Department. He could oversee paperwork until he was cleared to resume his job.

She reached down and stepped into her pants, pulling them over her hips. As soon as she snapped her jeans, she slipped her arms into the sleeves of her shirt, avoiding the mirror until she finished hooking the last button.

She straightened and looked into the reflective glass. What she saw made her flinch. Her black eyes made her look positively ghoulish. But it was her swollen mouth, evidence of Griff's thorough kisses, that drew her attention. Almost against her will, she lifted her fingers to her tender lips.

She didn't regret making love to him. It would be something she'd cherish the rest of her life.

But even in the face of never seeing him again, she knew she had to keep her emotions in check so he wouldn't suspect how much she was tempted to throw away the convictions that had taken a lifetime to build.

Would it be so bad to share Griff with his job? To plan a Christmas dinner and then eat by oneself?

A long-term relationship could lead to more than marriage. It could mean a child. She'd love to have Griff's baby.

As quickly as the thought came, she blanched. What if she was pregnant? When they'd made love before, she'd been safe because of the time of month. But what about now?

The numbers weren't lining up in her head.

What if she was pregnant?

A part of her wanted more than anything for that to be true.

And what about Griff?

He'd want the child. But what about her? She'd spent her entire youth feeling like unwanted baggage. Yes, her father loved her. But he hadn't wanted the responsibility of her.

She couldn't bear the idea of being an unwanted responsibility to Griff.

Maggie lowered her gaze from the mirror, feeling the dreadful weight of loneliness dragging down her shoulders.

Chapter 18

It was still dark when Griff woke in the small motel where he'd lived for three weeks following Mrs. Harris's arrest. He could have stayed in the boarding house, but he hadn't liked the idea of living under Mrs. Harris's roof another day, even if she was behind bars.

The sun was just starting to rise, and he swung his feet to the floor.

He had to find another place to live. The boarding house had been put up for sale to pay for Mrs. Harris's legal bills.

There was little he missed about his former lodgings. It had been merely a place to rest his head at the end of each day. The four pale green walls had never been a real home, which had suited him fine for the eight months he'd lived there.

He'd never wanted a home, believing it was better not to put down roots and build expectation.

But that was before Maggie.

Funny how he now associated the word "home" with Maggie.

He rubbed his head and reached for his pants. He should be looking forward to returning to active duty, but he wasn't.

Why?

Maggie. He couldn't stop thinking about Maggie.

He hadn't seen her since they'd left the cabin, and Mr. Beckwith and his wife had adopted Lucky.

According to Wylie, Maggie had left town two weeks ago, after the doctor gave her a clean bill of health.

Griff had promised to take care of the annulment, but he hadn't made any effort to initiate the proceedings.

First he'd made the excuse that he wanted to wait to get rid of his cast and he could drive his own car. But now, he admitted to himself that he hadn't made the effort because he didn't want a divorce or an annulment.

He lowered his face into his hands and rubbed his forehead. How many times would he relive every moment they'd spent together?

Each morning he awoke with the taste of Maggie on his lips, as he dreamed about making love to her. It wasn't until this morning that it suddenly occurred to him that they hadn't used any form of birth control.

Could Maggie be pregnant?

Maybe it was wishful thinking.

He hadn't brought birth control protection with him to the cabin. Hell, he hadn't needed it for months.

When they'd made love, he hadn't even thought about taking precautions.

He shook his head. How could he have been so irresponsible to put Maggie at that kind of risk?

He doubted that she'd been using any contraceptives. When would she have had time? They had been engaged and were an exclusive fictitious couple. Neither of them dated anyone else during those short months.

He envisioned in his mind's eye Maggie as a mother-to-be. She'd be beautiful. Soft and happy.

Griff lifted his head from his hands. Hope cut a swath through the despair he'd been fighting since they left the cabin.

If she was pregnant, they'd have to stay married. She didn't want to be a mother without her child having a father. Isn't that what she'd told him?

If they stayed married, then he'd have the time and proximity to make her fall in love with him.

For the first time in weeks, a slow honest-to-goodness smile broke out across his face. He hadn't felt so good since Maggie left.

Chapter 19

Two weeks later, Griff drove through the relatively quiet streets of Somerstown.

It had taken him a week longer than he'd planned to tie up all the loose ends in Pendleton.

After stopping at a convenience store to ask for directions, he found Maggie's shop situated between a souvenir store and a leather outlet.

He angle parked his Bronco and got out. The small community of ten thousand looked like the perfect place to settle down and have a family.

Walking up to the front door of the shop, he spotted the sign on the glass announcing the store's opening on Thanksgiving weekend, three weeks from now.

He knocked on the door and peered inside. When no one responded, he tried the door handle. It twisted easily beneath his grasp.

Making his way past a hodgepodge of wooden

boards, cartons of merchandise and a long counter with a cash register, Griff followed the hum of the sewing machine to a room toward the back of the building.

He stopped at the threshold and soaked in the sight of the woman who had haunted his dreams for too many weeks.

Maggie had foregone her usual man's styled shirt for a bright purple sweater and a pair of black knit pants that hugged the calves of her legs as she fussed over a porcelain doll nestled in her lap.

"Hi, Maggie."

He saw her swallow before she looked up. "Griff. What are you doing here?"

His gaze skimmed the loose-knit sweater. "Looking for you."

She set down her doll and stood up. "I'm not pregnant, if that's why you're here."

He blinked, having to take a moment to absorb the sudden pain. He exhaled slowly. "What makes you think that's why I'm here?"

"Because you knew neither of us used birth control and you wouldn't abandon an unborn child."

"You're sure about the pregnancy?"

The glimmer of sadness that flickered across her face gave him hope. "I took a pregnancy test and had my doctor check to confirm it. If I had been, I'd have told you."

Maggie forced herself to stay where she was as Griff digested the news. He didn't try to hide his disappointment. Griff was a man who needed a family, even if he didn't want to admit it.

"You could have called and saved yourself the trouble of driving here," she said.

"That wasn't the only reason I came."

"You wanted me to sign papers for the annulment?"

He took another step into the room, and she automatically moved back. "No."

"Are there problems?"

"Not in the way you mean."

"What then?"

He sighed and ran his fingers through his hair. "If you'd been pregnant, this would have been so much easier."

She wrapped her arms protectively over her stomach. "Easier? Why?"

"To convince you to marry me. For real."

Her sudden laugh sounded flat and humorless to her own ears. "Is that why you really came? Or do you just feel responsible?"

He didn't flinch. "Is that a 'no'?"

"Yes." She lifted her head and braced herself against the inevitable hurt of watching him walk out of her life for good.

"Good. That will give us plenty of time."

She blinked. "Time for what?"

"To make you fall in love with me?"

Love?

By the time she tested the word in her mouth, Griff had left the store.

Her mouth snapped shut as soon as she heard the door close behind him.

What game was he playing? Was he so desperate

to have a child, that he planned to seduce her into saying yes?

The sad thing was that she was desperately afraid she might agree, and they'd both end up paying the price.

Griff didn't return for the remainder of the day.

Maggie did her utmost to banish him from her thoughts and concentrate on the list of tasks she'd assigned herself. She had plenty to do before she opened the store.

After a late afternoon meeting with her accountant, she arrived at her small house on the edge of town and met her neighbor walking down the sidewalk.

"Hi, Maggie."

"Tanya, what are you doing here?" Maggie hoisted a few bags from her back seat. "Isn't this little Billy's choir night?"

The thirty-something apartment owner smiled. "Yes, but Bill Senior promised to take him so I could get the new renter of the house next door settled."

Maggie eyed the cottage-styled house on the other side of hers. "You've got a new renter?"

"Here he is now. Griff Murdock, meet Maggie Bennington."

Maggie's eyes widened then narrowed at the sight of the man carrying a suitcase in one hand and a bag in the other.

She didn't know why she should be surprised. She had suspected he was up to something. "What are you doing here?"

Tanya looked from one to the other. "You two know each other?"

"We're married," Griff said.

"Married?"

"Not for long," Maggie said.

"Oh, does that mean you don't want to rent the house, Mr. Murdock?" Tanya asked, not bothering to hide her bewilderment.

"Hopefully not for too long," Griff said.

Tanya hesitated, but when no one offered to enlighten her, said, "Well, let me know if you need anything. I'm just down the street."

As soon as her neighbor left, Maggie brushed past Griff and inserted the key into her lock.

He followed her inside.

She walked through the living room to deposit her bags on the wicker dining table as Griff checked out the interior.

"Nice house," he said. "It looks like you. Homey but classy."

She folded her arms. "Griff, this can't work."

"What can't work?"

"You and me." She had been rehearsing this in her mind ever since he'd shown up earlier today. "We were forced into an unnatural situation that caused—" she stumbled "—us to do things that we normally wouldn't have done."

"You don't think making love with your wife is normal?" He seemed amused.

She bit down on her lip. It wasn't right that she should be the one uncomfortable in her own house. Why did he have to be so stubborn?

"I'm not your wife," she said, with as much calmness and firmness as she could muster. "We can't continue this farce."

"I agree." He made no move to leave. Neither did he offer explanations. "What are you having for dinner?"

It was hard to think about food when he was standing so close. "I'll probably throw together a salad."

"Let me take you out for dinner."

He seemed determined to keep her off-balance. She could be equally as stubborn. "I don't think—"

He interrupted her. "You did most of the cooking when we were in the cabin, plus other things. Let me show you my appreciation."

It seemed churlish to refuse, but she didn't trust him. He appeared too relaxed and too confident for her peace of mind. "Are you going to badger me about marrying you?"

"We'll talk about anything you want."

For the next week, Griff didn't press her about marriage. Anytime she attempted to bring up about what his plans were, he became deliberately vague.

He seemed very interested in her shop and had even stopped by to help her construct wooden shelves for her display.

They either went out for dinner—his treat—or ate in her cozy dining room.

They were becoming too married-like, Maggie noticed, although they hadn't made love since they'd left the cabin.

And she didn't know how much more she could

take. Being with Griff, but not with him, produced an intense misery that increased each day.

You're in way over your head, Maggie. You've got to put an end to this before you start believing in the fairy tales that promised happily ever after.

Griff hadn't again mentioned his desire for making her fall in love with him. Nor had he said how long he planned to stay in town or anything about the annulment. Except for a fleeting kiss on her lips each evening before he left, their relationship had been strictly platonic. And it was starting to drive her crazy.

At the end of the week, she pulled her battered station wagon into her driveway and spotted Griff sitting on her porch.

Dressed casually in black jeans and a long-sleeved polo shirt, he looked much too delicious and uncop-like.

She wished her heart wouldn't leap at the sight of him. For a brief second, she rested her head against the steering wheel. She had fallen in love with him, and she didn't know how she was going to cope with her broken heart when he left.

She slowly got out of the car and walked up the sidewalk toward her house.

She loved her small bungalow-styled house. She'd spent the past few weeks decorating it with the odds and ends she'd collected throughout the years. But over the course of the past few weeks, she was beginning to realize the big three-cushion sofa, the wicker dinette set and her heirloom grandfather clock didn't add up to making her house into a home.

She was very much afraid only Griff could do that.

Would she ever look at the big chair in the corner of the living room and not picture Griff sitting there?

He had stamped his presence in her life, and she didn't know if she could ever erase him from her home or her heart.

Griff met her halfway. "I have a gift for you."

This cat-and-mouse courtship had to end sometime. It would be better to terminate the play sooner than later, before one of them got seriously hurt. Still, she tried to be gentle. "I don't need anything from you."

His smile contained a quizzical sadness. "Maybe not. But I need a lot from you, sweetheart, and I'm not giving up hope. Come over to my house, and I'll give you your present."

"Griff—"

"Trust me, you'll love it."

He left before she had a chance to respond.

What was she going to do?

She'd thought she'd had it all planned. The house, the shop and a future free from the pain of the past. She hadn't wanted to risk taking a back seat to a cop's career.

But was she willing to forsake those goals, if she could have a life with Griff?

She'd never been so tempted. Maintaining control over her goals had been what had made her life livable.

Now her world had tipped haphazardly on its axis.

When Griff arrived, he'd told her he wanted her to fall in love with him.

Did that mean he loved her?

She'd made make-believe the reality for her future. But suddenly she knew it would never be enough.

She wanted a real home with a man who would love her and give her children.

What would she have to sacrifice if that man was Griff?

Chapter 20

Maggie changed into a midcalf-length dress before she crossed her yard and approached Griff's house. Since she'd arrived in Somerstown, she'd rediscovered her love of wearing more feminine clothes. She enjoyed the swishing fabric against her body.

Walking up the steps, she saw Griff standing just inside waiting for her.

He stepped back to let her in. "I like the dress."

"Thank you."

She couldn't contain the nervous laugh at the absurdity.

"Something funny?" he asked.

"I just realized how much has changed in a few weeks. We're no longer Bennington and Murdock."

"Maybe we quit running from each other."

She turned and faced him. "Is that what we were doing? I thought we were both being safe."

"Yeah. And look where it got us?"

She was afraid to look too closely into the warm steel of his eyes. Did he want what she did, or was she creating more larger than life fantasies?

"Are you ready for your present?" he asked, before reaching for her hand and gently steering her toward the small parlor on the left.

The house Griff had rented still seemed curiously empty despite the fact he'd been living here for almost a week. Except for the furnishings that were already inside the house when he arrived, Griff hadn't bothered to add to its decor. He'd never said how long he planned to stay. But all indications told her it wouldn't be much longer.

At the threshold, he stopped her. "Close your eyes."

She did what he asked.

A few steps more, then he said. "All right. You can open them now."

She blinked and gasped.

Sitting on a long flat table stood a thirty-inch tall, cream-colored Victorian dollhouse.

Maggie had trouble comprehending what she was seeing. She circled the table before kneeling to peer into the patterned leaded windows that contained real metal. "Oh, Griff. It's perfect. Where did you get it?"

"I found it at a shop on the outskirts of Chicago. They had all kinds of fancy accessories, including chandeliers, but I thought you'd enjoy decorating it yourself."

She shook her head. "Why did you buy this?"

Griff reached for her hand and pulled her to her

feet. The heat of his skin caused chills to sweep through her as his arms went around her. "I love you more than I thought I'd ever love anyone in my life, Maggie. I can't promise that we can ever afford such a fancy house, but I want to spend the rest of my life bringing all your dreams to life. Will you marry me, Maggie, for real this time?"

"You're making this hard." She swallowed back the surge of tears that suddenly rose in the back of her throat. "What about your job? Pendleton is over an hour away."

"I handed in my resignation. I've been hired as the new police chief for Somerstown."

"But you loved your job."

"No. It was my safety net. It kept me from wanting more from life than I was given. That made it safe. But it was still just a job. I want you."

Maggie pulled her hand from his and stepped back. She couldn't think when they were this close. She could only feel Griff. She had to separate her feelings from the needy hunger.

"Do you love me, Maggie?" he asked.

The gruff tenderness in his voice brought her tears to the edge. "Yes, but I'm not sure it's enough."

"What would be enough?"

"I don't know." She turned her back on him so she could regain her composure. "I didn't expect you'd ever leave Pendleton or the department. The job was your life."

"I'm not your dad, Maggie."

No, he wasn't. But could she release the fears she'd held so long? "How do I know you aren't feeling responsible for me because I'm your partner's daughter?''

"I'm going to help you furnish that dollhouse," he said simply. "I figure it'll take a lifetime."

Maggie's gaze flickered back to his gift, and then returned to the strong emotion glimmering in his eyes. He was no longer shielding his feelings from her. He was asking her to believe in the dreams she'd always nurtured in her heart but never dared believe she'd have.

The world of make-believe would never be enough.

Could he see her heart in her eyes? "Marriage can be messy."

"My life can use a little clutter."

A lump rose in the back of her throat. "I'd never leave you," she said.

"I'd come after you if you did."

His arms beckoned and she couldn't deny herself any longer.

She rushed into the haven he offered, nestling against the muscled warmth and let the tears fall. "I wanted to be pregnant. I wanted to have our baby."

He held her as if he'd never let her go. "I know. But we'll have time to make lots of babies."

She lifted her head and reached up to touch his face. "I love you."

"Say it again."

"You first."

"Still don't trust me?"

She slipped her hands around his head. "I trust you to be with me every stormy night, sunny day and cloudy afternoon. But I need to hear the words, too."

"I love you, Maggie. Marry me."

She answered by pulling his face down to her and pressed her mouth to his. "All right. But it's your turn to wear the wedding dress."

The gray of his gaze gleamed down into hers. "I've got a better idea, how about we both get naked, Mrs. Murdock, and then flip for it?"

"With your two-faced coin?"

"Your powers of deduction never cease to amaze me."

"You're much too sure of yourself."

"Yeah, but you'll have plenty of time to train me. Now about that baby…"

Maggie sank into her husband's arms.

She'd tried to steel her heart against loving him, but Griff had broken through the bars she'd erected and taken her soul.

Maggie knew she'd never be truly alone again.

Epilogue

Griff pulled into the driveway in time to watch his young daughter boldly navigate the steps to greet him.

Eleven-and-a-half-month-old Selia Willow Murdock, her face screwed tight with utmost determination, had a profound fascination with any kind of staircase. She stubbornly refused her mother's assistance, even though Maggie stood close by in case her small daughter took a tumble.

Sheer contentment washed over him.

His wife and his daughter. Their love made his life complete and still humbled him.

Wylie often ribbed him about getting "stung" at his own wedding, but Griff couldn't be more content. He'd found a woman he'd love forever, and who amazingly loved him.

He'd finally managed to rise above the ashes of his past.

He knew he'd always worry about something happening to either Maggie or Selia. But he knew they'd never willingly leave him.

It had been two and a half years since he'd left his job in Pendleton and asked Maggie to make their marriage vows permanent.

The first year and a half of their life together hadn't been without pain. Maggie had gotten pregnant three months after their small intimate wedding in her living room. When she'd miscarried several weeks later, they both shed many tears. The pain of losing the unborn baby had been tough on them both, but their love had sustained them.

When Selia was born, he learned what real contentment was.

Maggie was a terrific mother and an incredible wife. After his daughter's birth, Maggie had hired their neighbor Tanya to manage the doll shop so Maggie could be home with the baby.

Selia finally conquered the last step, and Maggie scooped her up and gave her a big hug before pointing to Griff as he climbed out of his Bronco. "Look, sweetheart, Daddy's home."

His daughter reached out her hands to him. "Da," she squealed.

Griff intercepted his daughter. "How's my pretty girl? Have you been good to your mama today?"

Maggie winked. "She missed her daddy."

"How much?"

"I found her washing your socks in the bathroom toilet."

He chuckled, nuzzling the baby's ear, before leaning over to kiss Maggie. "Mmm, you taste good. How was your day?"

Maggie looped her arm through his as they strolled back to the house. "Wylie called."

"What did he want?"

"He asked if we wanted to meet him at the cabin this weekend."

"Did you tell him we want the bedroom?"

She smiled. "He'd agree to anything so long as he can spoil Selia."

"Then let's do it."

"Our bags are all packed."

With Selia in one arm and Maggie on the other, Griff didn't care where they spent the weekend. He had everything he needed or wanted right next to him. And he knew that wasn't going to change for the rest of his life.

* * * * *

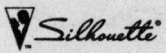

INTIMATE MOMENTS™
presents:
Romancing the Crown

With the help of their powerful allies, the royal family of Montebello is determined to find their missing heir. But the search for the beloved prince is not without danger—or passion!

Available in June 2002:
ROYAL SPY
by Valerie Parv (IM #1154)

Gage Weston's mission: to uncover a traitor in the royal family. But once he set his sights on pretty Princess Nadia, he discovered his own desire might betray *him*. Now he was determined to discover the truth about the woman who had grabbed hold of his heart....

This exciting series continues throughout the year with these fabulous titles:

Available only from Silhouette Intimate Moments at your favorite retail outlet.

Silhouette®
Where love comes alive™

Visit Silhouette at www.eHarlequin.com

SIMRC6

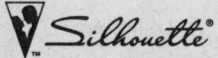

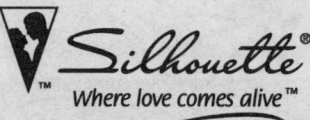

From award-winning author
MARIE FERRARELLA

Meet

Dr. Lukas Graywolf:
Lover, Healer and Hero in
IN GRAYWOLF'S HANDS
(IM #1155)
On Sale June 2002

Dr. Reese Bendenetti:
Lone Wolf, Doctor and Protector in
M.D. MOST WANTED
(IM #1167)
On Sale August 2002

Dr. Harrison "Mac" MacKenzie:
M.D., Bad Boy and Charmer in
MAC'S BEDSIDE MANNER
(SE #1492)
On Sale September 2002

Don't miss this exciting new series!
Available at your favorite retail outlet.

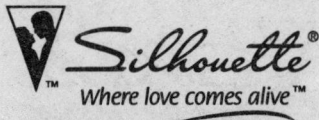

Where love comes alive™

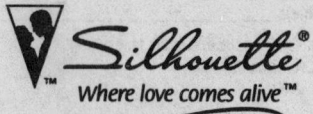